THE
INTERVIEW

RENAUD CONTINI

To my family and friends

THE INTERVIEW

It was already dark when R. came out of his office. 'The winter is arriving fast', he whispered to himself as he shut the exit door of the building sprawling its black tentacles behind him. On the way to the tram stop he whistled but the sound that came out was oddly artificial. It was as if R. had stolen the whistle from an overly trusting referee and blown into it later to consecrate his act of mischief. The few lonely souls he crossed paths with at that moment turned back towards him with perplexed glances but ultimately just shrugged and went their separate ways.

At the tram stop R. smiled continuously as he waited for the hopelessly familiar vehicle of transport. 'I don't know why I can't stop smiling. It's probably the nerves,' he observed to himself, absent-mindedly contemplating the skyscrapers on the opposite side of the street whose shapes were rendered formless by the onset of night. The rumbling sound of the approaching tram shook him off his reverie. He hopped on the second car and sat down next to an elderly lady with whom he exchanged no words at all because he knew that enterprise would be pointless.

'It is a pity she is so shy and reserved,' R. thought, 'particularly as today I have such excellent news to share.'

Thus constrained by the wasteland of excitement around him to keep the news secret, R. reckoned with complacency that nobody in that tram deserved hearing what he wanted to share. Those worthy of being told were few and far between even among the people who mattered in his life—his family and friends.

'Even with my loved ones, the titillating feeling of excitement might be spoilt at least a little bit if I told them straightaway,' R. remarked with a frown.

As he continued to talk to himself with trademark self-absorption, he did not notice that the elderly lady was now staring at him with an expression mingling curiosity and concern. She had an elongated forehead, a slightly hooked nose, and bright inquisitive grey eyes. She stood up and got off at the following stop.

'Who knows what on earth she's doing in the city all day long,' R. mused as he gazed through the window at the vanishing figure. Soon she took a right turn into a small alley and disappeared from view. 'I wonder if she lives in that little alley. This seems the most likely explanation for the regularity of her trips to that part of town. Or could it be that the sorceress read into my thoughts and went to give me away to my competitors? I ought to keep a close watch on her from now on,' he added with internal resolve and a forceful clenching of his fist.

Still R. could not resist picturing the traitorous acts that the grey-eyed lady might be guilty of performing at that very moment. In his mind's eye he saw her enter a badly lit café where men in suits were sipping on black tea, each one alone and pensive at his table. Each man was mysteriously eager to attract the newcomer's attention. Maybe the ageing woman was a renowned informant.

With careful steps she approached one of the men. She was wearing a cunning smile on her face that seemed to indicate she had already chosen him before she came in. The two nodded to each other and spoke briefly but the words they exchanged could not be heard. Only the look of satisfaction that steadily grew on the young man's face revealed his delight at the information he had just received.

'He knows!' R. exclaimed loudly in the tram. Some passengers, though not many of them, were alarmed by the sudden exclamation. They frowned to each other with a knowing look which was completely lost on R. It took him a long time to realise that he had only been dreaming; by the time he came to that conclusion at last, he had already arrived home.

His apartment was very simple, almost monastic. It had a tiny hall, a bathroom on the right, a kitchen in front, and a bedroom on the left. The place, which was very old, seemed to be undergoing a gradual process of decay. R. thought that if he touched one of the white walls the whole thing would crumble to pieces, so over time he became used to moving around nimbly between the different rooms without touching anything except the furniture.

It may seem strange that the thought never occurred to R. to move out of such a dreary environment, or that he even decided to move in at all. But he was tight with money, very tight, although by no means poor. His parents were of a middle-class background, his father an engineer and his mother a teacher. He had a well-paying job which allowed him to save sizeable amounts of money every month. But perhaps his intention was precisely to live in a cheap place lacking in comfort in order to save a great deal of money every month. For what long term purpose? R. was not sure about that. But he knew that at some point along the way, in the not so distant future, a purpose would emerge.

'My sanctuary!' he exclaimed with a sigh as he closed the entrance door behind him. He turned on the light in the hall and slipped to the bathroom to urinate. Another quirk of his was never to turn on the light in the bathroom. All he did was let the light of the hall penetrate into the bathroom by leaving the door slightly ajar. R. performed that strange action multiple times a day with the regularity of a clock because the mere idea of witnessing the decrepit state of the bathroom from close up, under an unforgiving light, filled him with deep anguish. The primary cause behind that anguish was symbolic. In a home, the place designated for cleaning ought to be kept clean.

'An impure bathroom means an impure body,' R. thought with a grimace.

His larger obsession with purity could be discerned in the fact that he owned no personal furniture. He had inherited what he had in the apartment entirely from the previous tenant, accepting it with arms wide open and even nonchalance. To complete the arsenal of the postmodern ascetic, R. also boasted few belongings.

However, since the apartment appeared to be on the verge of collapse, R. did not dare to give the bathroom the thorough cleaning it needed. Instead he contented himself with delicately scrubbing the floor, toilet and bathroom once a week. Evidently such a measure was not sufficient to remove all the stains, and the prospect of encountering big dirty spots all around him made his skin crawl. Luckily R. realised one night that the light in the hall enabled him to feel his way around the bathroom while shielding his eyes from chance encounters with the surrounding grime.

Having relieved himself in the dark, R. paced back to his bedroom and sat down at his desk. The bedroom was by far the biggest room in the apartment, with a surface area that covered more than half of the whole space. It was equally old and dilapidated. The walls had a hard, grainy texture that made R.'s hand bleed every time he rapped against them during a tantrum. The excrescence looked like a sea of deformed plaster, or a colony of tiny gargoyles. Their smudged whiteness contrasted with the austerely functional desk of black wood that R. used mostly for his computer and his books.

As a would-be ascetic R. owned very few books, ten or twelve at most. Most were works of philosophy by the likes of Kierkegaard and Schopenhauer. There were also some classic Russian and French novels, and even treatises of economics, although those looked suspiciously shiny and pristine, like a basket of fresh fruits left entirely untouched by their carnivorous owner. By contrast the philosophy books appeared much worn out.

'I need to make at least one phone call,' R. sighed with noticeable impatience. 'I can't go to bed not having shared the news with at least one person.'

With a brusque movement he grabbed his phone from the desk and looked blankly at the screen, wondering about who to contact. His mind laboriously began to piece together a vague list but struggled to keep the burgeoning representation within a unified frame, so it frittered away without warning. Not intent on giving up anytime soon, R. decided to make a random pick among a select group of people close to his heart.

It was his mother that made the lucky draw. R. flung himself on the low, creaky bed behind him and lay down, staring at the ceiling for a few minutes. He still had his phone in hand and his thumb ready to press the button to call his mother whenever he should decide to so do. As he continued to muse his thumb muscles became a little strained but the pain occasioned by the strain was muted by a parallel feeling of mounting excitement. Slowly but surely a wave of excitement rushed through his bones as the idea of sharing the prized information with his mother solidified in R.'s mind.

The only counter thrust to that wave was a fragment of stubbornness refusing to die, the word of caution he had spoken to himself against divulging too much too quickly. It was not mere superstition, nor the complacency of the man who knows a secret and silently relishes the special power he possesses over the information it contains. R. knew that he had deeper reasons for wanting to use words sparingly, although at that moment he just knew without being able to translate his knowledge into words. It was as if that knowledge was possessed not by his head but by his heart.

After two unsuccessful tries, his mother finally answered the phone. To his astonishment R. found it much harder to contain himself than he had expected. After briefly asking his mother how she had been doing lately he quickly found a way of shifting the topic of conversation to the object that had prompted him to call in the first place.

'I have been invited to an interview,' he said to her with a grin as wide as it was invisible to his mother. However, as soon as he had uttered those words and without waiting to hear his mother's reaction, R. hastened to specify that he would not be able to say anything more about the interview. As a justification he simply invoked a 'confidential matter'.

Ms. C. expressed her delight about the piece of news but respectfully took care not to probe her son any further, as per his request. A reserved but astute psychological observer, she knew how sensitive R. was but also how inflexible he could become when he felt that a promise had been betrayed. Thus she remained uninquisitive both to please her son and in order not to risk losing him. Deep inside she felt great relief about the unexpected opportunity, because she knew that her son had been unhappy with his current position for a long time. She favoured the idea of his changing jobs rather than quitting and facing unemployment. She firmly believed in the power of work to structure life.

The two of them chatted for a little while, mostly about mundane topics forgotten almost as soon as they were covered. In particular R.'s mother asked him about his next visit to the south. With a wistful wave of the hand that only he and his mirror perceived, R. replied that he had been craving the Mediterranean sun as a cure for the bleakness of the weather in his part of the continent. But although he complained and even said that he would hop on the nearest train if he could, he solemnly reminded his mother about the new demands made on him by the interview.

'The stakes are high. I cannot take that risk,' R. said. As if to thwart his mother's anticipated response he insisted that he did not want to talk about the interview anymore—at least 'not for now'.

It was his mother's turn to smile her invisible smile. It was a smile that both paid heed to what she heard and meant to reassure the worrier. Of course she wouldn't repeat anything to anyone. She knew that her son knew, because otherwise he would never have talked to her about that interview, not in a million years.

R. did not think he would return to the family home before the Christmas holidays, although he chose to remain evasive on the matter during the conversation with his mother. Christmas was only two months away, and until then he could count on his brother to visit Ms. C. from time to time. He convinced himself of that, in any case, with his powerful ability for imaginative projection. In doing so he conveniently omitted as if through a magical spell that his brother hadn't visited the family home in months. Like so many faculties of the human cognition, imagination is not infinite and must sink into the void after drifting about for a while. Many of the philosophy books that R. had studied explored precisely that topic   finitude and the mind.

Not very long after he had tried, more or less unconsciously, to rid himself of the guilt associated with his infrequent visits to his mother by deflecting responsibility onto his brother, R. suddenly remembered that his brother was even more solitary and self-absorbed than he himself. It did not matter that K. still lived and worked down south and was only a thirty minute drive away from the family house. As soon as K. began to interpret any plan as a duty, he would lose all motivation to commit to it. R. knew that trait of K.'s personality very well—in fact it was perhaps K.'s most reliable trait. However, before entering into more detail about the confusing personality of K., to whom R. was both close in some respects and distant from him in others, it is more pressing at this minute to dwell on R.'s own complex and not entirely readable character.

The few seconds during which R. managed to forget about his brother's habit of not visiting the family home made him feel the powerful relief that a hidden compensation would replace the absence of his own. Quickly, however, relief gave way to shock at the absurdity of the patent fantasy. The brief moment of open-mouthed elation was interrupted suddenly by heart palpitations and shivers down the spine so strong they actually hurt him.

'What the hell was I thinking,' R. muttered to himself in a tone of reproach. He sighed and tapped his forehead lightly as he came to the ineluctable conclusion, like the little black square at the end of a logical proof, that neither he nor his brother would visit their mother during the next two months. He tried to assess how upset his mother would be but was forced to admit that certain phenomena cannot be quantified.

'At least she will be able to visit granny, since they live so close to each other. There could be numerous visits,' he reckoned, smiling. Eventually he decided to keep the door open to the possibility of one short visit on his side—but only on the condition that the interview be over by then. At last he felt satisfied.

This was an archetypal illustration of R.'s typical process of reasoning. He would begin by bathing comfortably in a short-lived illusion, itself the outgrowth of his dreamer's tendency to live in an internal world. Sooner or later the dagger of reality would strike him out of nowhere and critically injure him. The seriousness of the mental wound suffered at that moment would be a hundred times worse than warranted by the gravity of the banal situation R. had been keeping aloof from; but due to his sleepy lack of foresight, the outcome would be unfolding crushingly in front of him in its already final form. Eventually, at the price of much psychical effort R. would manage to reach a makeshift compromise, neither satisfying nor worrisome.

Perhaps R.'s curious proclivities will appear like nothing very odd. When a vivid imagination combines with neurotic traits, behaviours of that kind are not uncommon. However, in R.'s case this triadic relationship with reality, consisting in oblivion following by shock and compromise, had come to colour his existence so deeply that he truly seemed at times to organise his life around it. Even within the confines of his seedy apartment he would sometimes sit on his bed and look around musingly for minutes on end, lost in his daydreams, then suddenly gasp with fright: 'This place is falling apart! One day the ceiling is going to collapse on my head and crush me!' But after a few minutes of extreme anxiety the storm would gradually subside.

Laboriously R. would grope his way back to compromise. 'I'm staying here because the rent is so cheap. I'm saving incredible amounts of money every month. No other apartment would afford me that luxury,' he would say to himself, inwardly chucking at his pun on the word 'luxury'. He reckoned with a tingling spine that if by some unlucky accident the ceiling should collapse one night and flatten him to the size of a wafer, then fate shall have spoken. 'I don't particularly enjoy this life anyway,' he would add with great conviction.

However, this conviction had weakened dramatically since the news of the interview. This led R. to ask himself on the twice daily walks between the tram stop and his office, under the pouring October rain sticking like fresh makeup to the city of ___, whether only those with a reason to live are afraid of death. It struck R. as obvious that the answer was no. Most people fear death, although they would be utterly incapable of describing or even identifying their life purpose. What does not exist can neither be described nor identified.

Strikingly, it is often the people who admit candidly to lacking a purpose in life that display the greatest contentment with the repetitive grind of work, family and

11

leisure. But there is worse: even the world's unhappiest souls fear death too much to terminate their wretched existences. They effectively choose misery over the release from misery. Humanity—what a perplexing group of beings! Those too were R.'s thoughts. He confessed to a certain dishonesty in claiming that he would not mind his head being crushed to pieces by the ceiling's collapse. In a sense the ceiling would be doing the job for him, wouldn't it? It would save R. from the need to actually commit suicide by himself like a big boy. Perhaps it is only in the latter case that a man is allowed to speak of surmounting the fear of death. Seizing the dark shadow of death with one's own hands is an incomparably greater feat than merely creating the conditions for a fatal accident.

Sometimes R. would not just have those thoughts but feel a misplaced pride at the realisation that he was capable of such complex thinking. Although he wouldn't have admitted it to himself, he saw himself as a person of profundity in an ocean of shallow opportunism, insipid afterwork parties and duplicitous friendliness barely covering up an obsession with professional advancement. Most of the people he knew in ___ were acquaintances but none were friends. 'The people who live here are persons with an a, *personas*,' R. wrote once on a slip of paper upon returning home after an especially frustrating day. First he contemplated the little piece of witticism with great satisfaction. Alas, that momentary pleasure was soon drowned in the banality of its source.

R. tossed the slip of paper into the bin with an expression of disgust on his face. The advantage of passing thoughts over written notes is that thoughts cannot be tossed into bins; they are too evanescent to be analysed and taken apart as an outcome of the analysis. Thus it is possible for a self-important but stupid person to remain cosily self-important, since the shallowness of their thoughts possesses an intangible quality which renders them mystifyingly slippery. The irony is that those mystifying ideas are condemned to remain shallow in order not to crumble like a castle of cards struck by a gust of wind.

In R.'s defense he had at least the courage of writing many of his thoughts down. In this way he was able to filter the superficial bits of prose from the more intriguing ones. From his teenage years he had dreamt of becoming of writer, but not just any writer. R. wanted to write ambitious books from a literary viewpoint, but also, if possible, to be able to live from his books. As this alignment of the stars was extremely rare in contemporary society he prioritised the first goal at the expense of the second, and found himself working at an office job in the city of ___ by his mid-twenties, keeping up writing on the side and officially 'just as a hobby'. He had excelled at university and been able to secure an enviable position with a human rights organisation well-known the world over, a fact which tickled his ego a little bit and provided the initial momentum that his young career needed.

Within that organisation R. had been working for years in the social media unit of the communications department and over the years had quietly become a respected member of staff. What the other members of staff ignored was R.'s secret distaste for them. He covered up that distaste very well but it was profound. Perhaps the fact that it was buried so deep inside his heart allowed that distaste to remain covered up. As for the reasons behind it, they will become clearer in the course of this narrative, but can't be clarified right now, because right now the words would not capture those reasons. Just in the same way that a painting requires a background frame, R.'s covert contempt for his colleagues requires the frame of this narrative not to come across as simply callous and petty.

R. enjoyed philosophical thoughts because he considered his colleagues—'the others', as he liked to call them—incapable of such questionings. Thus he kept his passion alive, bolstering his resilience to an increasingly alienating world, albeit sometimes at the cost of appearing insane. But then, out of nowhere, like a guardian angel materialising suddenly in front of him, R. had heard the news about the interview. Who would have expected him to be shortlisted? Certainly not himself, although his hopes in that regard had been equal in size to his fatalism.

'I absolutely must not tell anyone at work about the interview,' R. thought to himself as he opened the door to the ground floor of a tall glass building in the shape of a capsizing ship. Yet it was called the Petal Building—an ill-fitting name given it for arcane reasons that nobody knew about, but which turned out over time, for equally impenetrable reasons, to be rather fitting. There was nothing outstandingly flower-like about that building except that the interior was densely populated with plants. It was situated right next to the train tracks. On the other side of the tracks were a number of United Nations buildings dotting the cityscape all the way down to a large lake of crystal blue.

A little park circled the Petal Building. Although un-assuming in itself, its being the only park around that part of town immediately endowed it with great signifi-cance in the eyes of the people working there. Nobody ever seemed to use the benches, under the grip of a per-vasive fear that the planks of wood would crack under the pressure of anxious bodies. By contrast the stray dogs were far less picky and enjoyed roaming through the park in the morning. Since the Petal Building was entirely made of glass those old, sickly dogs could be seen limping around through the walls at every moment by the em-ployees inside. Their failing health was obvious and clashed nastily with the bureaucratic atmosphere that sat-urated the interior of the building. In the stolen expressions of his coworkers R. recognised the hidden de-sire for the dogs to be put down. 'They do not fit here, they are so ugly, their dirty bodies are failing,' the faces seemed to say.

Of course such paraphrases were not the truth but R.'s interpretations of what he saw in those faces. Many of them were not expressive at all; indeed it was their pride not to be. A noble cause like the defense of global human rights has little room for ego, at least in appearance. It is better for the human rights defender to imagine himself as a tiny cog working towards a cause much larger than the scope of his own fleeting and whimsical desires.

R.'s organisation was located on the four floor of the Petal Building. He slipped quietly into the lift with low-ered head and pressed the button. At the last second a tanned hand inserted itself between the closing doors and forced them open. A woman in her thirties greeted him

15

with a smile half hiding an apology, and pressed another button. She seemed to be of Indian origin but R. remained cautious with his conclusions because he knew how multicultural the city of ___ was despite its small size. He was quite familiar with her but only by sight, never speech. Whenever they ran into each other it was as if some transparent tape was suddenly glued to their lips, sealing them.

R. reflected that he would like to invite her on a date in the event, not realised so far, that he found the courage to talk to her. All the approaches he was currently able to contemplate were formal. Yet he had never seen her with another man despite how eager her eyes looked. Maybe she kept that eager look specially for R. without him knowing because he did not pay attention to how she looked at other men. True, her beauty was not that of a Greek statue. She had a slightly snub nose and her smiles, when you looked carefully at the entire cycle of their unfolding, had the curious habit of distorting into pouts. To counteract those blemishes she had gorgeous black hair flowing and shining like a river of melted graphite, as well as healthy round cheeks screaming love of life. Her elegance was subdued on the surface but bright underneath. Most strikingly she exuded a fiercely human kind of warmth indescribable in mere words but radiant with vulnerable openness.

'We would be a happy couple in a heartless world,' R. fantasised without shame as the woman was still posted right next to him waiting to get to her floor. Her penetrating hazel eyes were looking at him and he was looking at them. Why not talk to her? Who can tell?

Some people we love to love in our dreams but not outside of those dreams, and it is a sad fact of life that from a coldly statistical standpoint those peculiar relationships usually last longer than the real ones. Sometimes R. asked himself whether they might even outlast death and endure in heaven.

R. came out of the lift on the fourth level and raced straight to the office. He was not late but on the verge of it, in that strange in-between where anxiety spurs us to accelerate for no rational reason. As the entire office space was partitioned with glass everyone could see what everyone else was doing. 'At least they can't see inside my mind,' R. mused facetiously. It is impossible to give a clear idea of how much R. relished the fact nobody could guess his thoughts. The mere possibility of a traitorous musing sent him to the heights of ecstasy, because he knew that he could not be caught. If he wanted he could shake hands with his manager in a few minutes' time whilst internally obsessing over handing in his resignation, preferably at a busy time of year when the organisation would be most in need of him. What a treat to be capable of letting these people down at least in concept!

On the way to his office desk R. ran into his manager, Mr. Axel, who welcomed him with his moist handshake and suspicious smile. Another of the man's distinctive traits was the manner in which his unsuccessful jokes were always clothed in a robe of simulated hilarity. As a result the audience would laugh, either because Mr. Axel's own laugh was infectious or because the junior staff dreaded to know how he coped with silence. That risk was all the more impossible to envisage taking because Axel never looked annoyed. He was always smiling. So whenever his face assumed a merely normal expression, neither happy nor sad, his colleagues were naturally inclined to think him very sad and preoccupied. But since they dreaded to know how he coped with silence they continued to enable his joking and laughing; as a fact of life, risk has to be taken very seriously even with the most apparently harmless people. Besides, there was a sinister element to Axel's constant good nature because human beings are not usually constant in their behaviour. It was as if Axel had failed at failure, the lot of humanity, and as a result he paradoxically seemed less of a human.

He was only a few years older than R., a high achiever with bright green eyes and almost entirely bald. But his baldness was not a handicap, on the contrary it gave him the youthful look that bald men usually only get to enjoy in their fifties. By contrast, from certain angles Mr. Axel almost resembled a baby. His tendency to sputter during his punchlines only reinforced that impression.

As he grabbed R.'s hand to shake it softly he said hello and, not waiting for a response, immediately informed R. that Martina, the human resources secretary, was in bed with fever. 'But I do wonder, who is this lucky guy called Fever?' he almost shouted at R. Predictably his mouth shot bullets of saliva like a laser pistol, but R. had learned agility with time and dodged the bullets.

'I will see you in my office in half an hour, as planned,' Axel suddenly added in tone of great earnestness. Switching on and off at lighting speed between light-heartedness and gravitas was another of Axel's odd traits.

Still, R. did not actually mind him that much. He appreciated Axel's absence of cruelty, an absence so complete that R. used to think only angels were capable of achieving it. True, Axel never dared to question the director's choices. For this reason he never seemed to wield much power; the organisation almost had to recruit sheepish-looking interns on purpose to ensure they would respect Axel's authority. A highly competent yet ego-driven recruit would have crushed the poor buffoon in a couple of days. R. sat somewhere in the middle, neither sheepish nor competent, and so possessed within himself the elements of compromise.

Axel wielded the modest powers he had with enthusiasm and diplomacy, especially with the partners of the organisation for whom, as the head of external relations, he was the main point of contact. These people would laugh at his jokes and do so sincerely, as R. eventually came to realise. Familiarity with the lay of the land in the international world explained why that phenomenon was not a miracle but an essential ingredient in the diplomat's day to day. Multilateral diplomacy is a realm of pretense, where the form of the message delivered matters a hundred times more than its content. Sometimes the content does not even matter because both parties already agree on it implicitly, a case often encountered in exchanges between members of NATO or the deceased Warsaw Pact.

Now in the field of human rights that logic of pretense reaches its extreme application. Even a tiny step back should allow anyone to perceive the anomalous status of the city of ___ as the informal capital of human rights. ___ is located in the world's richest country by most measures; while as a city it is extremely wealthy due to the financial investment it attracts. While the quality of its democratic institutions is to be commended, the legitimacy of its title as the global seat of human rights does not thereby follow. To speak plainly, could not such a seat be a little more representative of the countries and regions that it is mandated to support? The answer is yes and barely requires thinking. Sadly, however, western governments prefer to fund organisations staffed by individuals who look, act, and laugh like them. Mr. Axel happens to be one such individual. A shower of meteors could not flatten a mountain with the same ruthlessness as mistrust of the global south does the temperaments of Western politicians and diplomats.

After that brief exchange with Mr. Axel, R. waved at a few more colleagues on the way to his office. It was an unremarkable office, small and rectangular as befitted the average middle employee. Two wooden desks faced one another, glued like Siamese twins in a sea of cobalt blue. A few low shelves and a printer occupied the corners while two tall exotic plants bordered the desks on both sides. Like everywhere else on Level 4 the floor was made of blue carpet, the furniture of a light grey colour with the exception of the wooden desks, while the partitions and windows were all impeccably transparent. Although a few years old, the Petal Building had been designed in such a silly way that it was impossible to open the windows. One felt permanently outdoors on good days, caged in a prison of glass on bad ones. During absent-minded interludes R. would often hum the melody of Blondie's song 'Heart of Glass', which he liked very much, though on those occasions he observed that the building itself lacked that mythical heart.

'If only things had more of a pulse around here,' R. reflected.

Since the workspace had no windows but only glass walls, very little air circulated and the staff had to bring their own bottles of water to avoid headaches caused by the abnormal ambient heat. The reflection of the sunbeams through the glass turned Level 4 into a microwave even during the autumnal months. For the artful employees the only viable strategy was to lower the blinds and spend their days in the half darkness. As a practitioner himself R. had found the outcome more bearable than expected. In a paradoxical way the darkness added a layer of intimacy to the faceless environment of the Petal Building.

Upon settling down at his desk R. was politely greeted by Milena, the personal assistant to the director of communications who sat in front of him. Her brown curly hair fell down her shoulders and almost covered her curved lips constantly surrounded by dimples. From the first encounter with that Italian woman R. had been mesmerised by the contrast between the seriousness of her expression and the ease with which those dimples formed in the middle of her cheeks whenever a smile was about to be offered. Most of the time the smile was not offered because Milena was avaricious but it was too late and the dimples bounced out of her cheeks all the same.

R. located a sense of mystery in that contrast and found that mystery attractive. Although fleeting, the attraction R. felt had an anchor in the fact that just like him Milena had a university degree in philosophy. During their first conversation he had almost cried, ecstatic, when

Milena had dropped the name of Schopenhauer and developed a train of thought that R. could no longer recall.

It is unfortunate that time shouldn't be the kind of entity that knows how to hide. Only a few more serious interactions were sufficient for R. to realise that Milena was not the sort of nymph he had envisioned. Her tendency to cling to conventional opinions was frankly extreme and only surpassed by her anxiousness to look good with the top management. The existential disease she suffered from was that widespread condition of the human psyche who must remain alien to individual thought no matter the context at hand. The context does not matter because the entire soul is banal. 'Give me a risky idea and I will crush it with my mallet,' Milena's gentle eyes seemed to say.

But Milena's soft backbone was not the trait what bothered R. the most. He resented her duplicity far more, especially the effortless ease with which Milena would turn into her boss's private snitch at a moment's notice. Her skills in that area were so refined—they flirted with the virtuosic. Every plaintive word uttered in that office seemed somehow to make its way into the director of communications' sharp ears.

One instance in particular had driven R. to the brink of fury. One morning, having overslept a little, he had skipped breakfast and hurried to work. Around the corner from the tram stop a bakery wafted to him the sweet smell of fresh pastries. With expertly coordinated movements he bought two croissants almost without stopping and strode on to the office. Sitting down at his desk with anticipatory delight he greeted Milena without looking at her, took out the chocolate-filled croissants and ate them with relish while reading the news on his laptop.

This should have been a completely forgettable anecdote, except that the next day R. was summoned to the director of communications' office.

'You can't eat breakfast in your office after 9AM,' warned the gigantic lady whose doll-like face failed to match her body. 'Keep in mind that you are paid for this job,' she admonished him further in a confusing tone of cold, jarring indifference.

Midway through that last sentence she had already turned back to her emails. With an almost imperceptible wave of the hand she called the situation a 'non-event' and pointed casually at the door to indicate the way out.

R. fumed in silence as he exited his tormentor's office. A non-event! Since when did non-events require humiliating discipline? Whatever the method of eating a croissant, that fact taken in itself can only be insignificant, but a person—and even more radically, an organised group of people—is capable of injecting meaning into inert matter. In this way five minutes of the daily work of a nondescript baker can be turned into an object of searing condescension. R.'s mood worsened even further when as his anger began to cool down the realisation dawned on him that the director of communications could not have known about the croissants without the help of an informer. From that realisation it was easy and painful to infer that Milena had been the informant, since she alone had witnessed the scene apart from R. himself.

R. clenched his fists as he now stared at the young woman with the eyes of death, nearly breaking his pen to pieces. In a society without laws or police he would have ripped out her glasses and forced them down her throat, but fear and his superego forbade him to do that. To put Milena on the spot would be pointless—she would never confess, she was too proud. She would stress the transparency of the walls and the director of communications' quasi-supernatural field of vision.

'It's about twice as wide as any regular human field,' she would say.

Maybe she wouldn't say those things which were figments of R.'s imagination but all the same, she would choose denial. The enterprise was not only hopeless but dangerous, since by confronting her R. would give Milena the keys to future intimations of acute paranoia against him but obtain only a fistful of sand in return.

That episode had convinced R. that he could trust no one at the office. To that new form of defiance was added growing disillusionment with the futility of his line of work and the slowly emerging lie about what his organisation drew its income from. It was a lie as yet uncovered in its substance but the first step, pointing the finger at it and no longer moving, had been achieved by R.

Sometimes he asked himself very basic questions. What were his colleagues doing at their desks all day long? Of course there were staff meetings but those usually resembled giant linguistic jigsaws more than meetings. Visioning seminars, brainstorming sessions, advocacy workshops, field visits to nebulous fields—

those labels meant nothing to him and he wondered what kind of magic potion the others must have drunk to create some meaning from nothing. He also inevitably wondered why he himself has not been offered to drink it, and from there a whole sequence of tortured thoughts followed. It did not help that R. was too intelligent for his job. Maybe his whole predicament was summed up in that observation, but his buried lack of self-esteem was not buried enough and still shielded his eyes from it.

Of course he knew the tasks that his position involved since he performed them every day and scarcely ever deviated from them. He worked as a communications officer in the division of external relations; his area of expertise was the tailoring of messages to the organisation's partners and donors. But somewhere along the assembly line he would lose sight of the tiny works of art he had tailored. As attached files they would be swallowed in Mr. Axel's long list of emails and who knew what their future looked like—R. had not the least notion. And although he used to ask he quickly stopped doing that because the organisation he worked for, despite its medium size, was more hierarchical than a Soviet department. Hierarchy and snitches were held in common, nobody doubted that. But as a result R. suffered from structural blindness of sight to the purpose of his own work and whenever asked about his job, felt like the most inarticulate little cog in the big machine.

When he finally sat at his desk that morning, R. was assailed by the burning temptation to tell Milena about the interview. He only managed to stop himself thanks to contrary and even more powerful thoughts revolving round his mind. The envisioned pleasure would be multiplied a hundredfold once he had secured the news of his success, but for that he had to wait and keep his fingers crossed. The interval could still be filled with daydreams, and so R. daydreamed about the day when he would drag his feet on purpose to get to work, purchase two enormous chocolate croissants on the way and gobble them voraciously close to Milena's face. On the heels of the ineluctable snitching he would be summoned to the gigantic lady's office, but that time he would draw his sword from his sheath with glee and announce his resignation in favour of a 'better' job whose six letters he would meticulously draw out in a taunting drawl. The intense joy that he would feel, stemming from emotional release, would be in direct proportion to his months and months of mounting frustration.

'Don't forget about the meeting with Axel,' Milena reminded R. in her jarring Italian accent.

The irritant was not the Italian sound of her tongue but the casualness with which she disdained the very idea of trying to sound non-Italian. With staggering constancy she kept strewing the stresses over all of the wrong syllables. Sometimes the stresses would be scattered so chaotically that R. would not have the slightest idea what Milena was saying.

'You're an absent-minded professor,' she teased him with a full display of her dimples.

'Don't worry, I haven't forgotten,' R. answered while rummaging through a bundle of files. He rarely minded a conversation but his timing often clashed with the internal clocks of others and only on the best of days was he able to properly multi-task.

'You'll be discussing the components of the Mali project,' Milena continued dreamily, wrongly placing the stress on the first syllable of the word *component*—one of her recurring mistakes and also the most abhorrent to R. Half-concealed by his files he winced with whatever discretion he could muster.

The meeting went as expected. From it R. learned nothing tangible, only another batch of eye-grabbing slogans such as 'Peace is Possible' and 'The Moment for Mali'. For a good chunk of it Axel moderated a discussion between two Bamako-based programme officers who had been doing interviews with randomly picked Malians about what peace and human rights meant to them, and compiling the information into a big file. R. wished he wasn't caricaturing the two officers in his mind by having those thoughts, but in fact nothing else could be safely ascertained about their work from the discussion they were having. Of course they peppered their talk with mentions of workshops, campaigns, meetings and brainstorming sessions. Those words were like thick white clouds through which nothing could be seen but only the milky surface that whetted people's appetites.

When the meeting ended Axel patted R. on the shoulder and asked him how the 'wordsmith' was doing, meaning R. himself. Axel loved to flatter his colleagues with quick, one-word compliments that didn't hang around in the ambient atmosphere for too long. He didn't think very often but his gut told him that the best way to sound sincere in flattery was to use wit, and then quickly move on as if nothing had happened. R. shrugged his shoulders inwardly.

'If only I wasn't so damn perceptive,' he observed to himself, feeling tedium already creeping over him. He re-assured his manager in an equally uninspired fashion, as the bar being set so low did not motivate him to try harder.

'I have come up with ideas on how to expand our funding base for the Mali project from a communications perspective,' R. said to Axel. 'I will liaise with the fundraising department and share the key messages I am about to develop for our next campaign. Hearing the programme officers share their first-person experiences in the field has been useful in this regard.'

Alex nodded with a smile so warm that if he had spoken, honey would have to come out of his mouth. In his own fashion R. had become a master of the art of saying nothing substantial with studied eloquence.

*****

Fidgeting in his office chair, R. spent the last five minutes before close of business counting the seconds to the hour of release. From that time onwards it was acceptable to leave, according to the invisible rules of the organisation. R. was amused to observe how the other employees were always so anxious to stick around for as long as possible just to impress their managers. It was a rather vulgar strategy, he thought, and one that he had uncovered more than once as disingenuous. Let a day happen when the managers had to leave the office early and everyone would be gone five minutes later.

'I should have brought my hat with me,' R. said out loud in a disgruntled tone as a heavy raindrop splashed on top of his skull en route to the tram stop.

The fact he had even forgotten the precious item surprised him given how bad the weather was in ___ around that time of the year. Fortunately a pleasant sense of anticipation soon overtook him, the drunkenness associated with his next thought. He was going on a date! When was the last time he had been on a date? Well, perhaps not as long ago as his selective memory led him to believe, but that date was a thrilling prospect compared to all the previous dates he had already forgotten about, because the woman he was about to meet had no idea that it was a date. In his bored man's brain it was more than a date; it was a mission.

She was a Swiss woman of Uruguayan descent called Elsa. R. had made her acquaintance during an internship that they had done together for a United Nations agency, although since then Elsa had abandoned that career path to return to studying. In the last two years Elsa had become R.'s good friend, sometimes even his confidante, but of late R. had begun noticing a growing frustration in him whenever he called her to mind. He came to the conclusion that he desired her and that his frustration came from not being able to enjoy her body but only her mind. We can figuratively make love to our friends' minds but not to their bodies. If we do, this changes the essence of the friendship, whereas matters of the mind don't. Maybe this says something about the question of mind-body dualism.

Buoyed up by the news of the interview, R. decided that it was time to tell Elsa about his romantic interest. It would have been better to hear Elsa confess her own interest first, but R. kept running after the hope of that confession without ever witnessing its materialisation. Perhaps Elsa's signals required mastery of a foreign language inaccessible to him. Perhaps she only wanted to be his friend. In fact, R. himself was unsure of the depth of his feelings. He sometimes wondered if boredom was not the main reason for his wanting to fall in love with Elsa.

This time, R. had to use several means of transport to get to his destination. The tram brought him to the central train station where he hopped on a bus to a lively area near the lake called the ___. Wedged in between the international and financial districts, it was the only multicultural neighbourhood in the city and even boasted a night life. But that night the pouring rain was keeping everyone locked inside the cafés and bars. R. had to cross the entire neighbourhood across its breadth to get to the café where he was to meet Elsa. The rain was indefinitely killing the atmosphere around the ethnic restaurants and that spoilt the pleasure R. usually felt in strolling down the central avenue. Speeding forward from awning to awning he paid no attention to the animated crowds massed together like contorted shapes behind the flashing windows that dotted the street on both sides.

Halfway through his journey a massive downpour forced him to seek refuge under an awning chosen at random from the row to his left. It sheltered the entrance to a little hall giving access to an old apartment complex. R. tried but failed to see the inside because the light in the hall flickered and was covered in dirt. Cigarette butts and empty beer bottles were strewn about the floor right next to the door.

'It feels almost like a different city,' R. muttered under his breath. He looked at his watch and nodded. 'I'm a little early anyway.'

He turned around and gazed pensively at the pouring rain. Recoiling at the idea that he was wasting his time, he conjured different scenarios for the date with Elsa and tried to assess his objective chances for romance. Amused and hopeful, R. weighed the options in his mind; then he weighed them in his heart too. His favourite poet, Paul Verlaine, visited him in his thoughts.

'It rains in my heart like it rains on the town,' he hummed, accompanied by the music of tiny splashes.

Suddenly R. felt the sting of a presence next to him. His muscles strained and inside his body his bones began to shiver. He didn't know whether to ask if someone was there or just to wait until the illusion dissipated. That surplus of options left him paralysed and barely able to think. He could not tell what the nature of that sting was because he had neither heard nor seen anything, and yet there had definitely been a sting. The physical reaction of his body was there to testify to it.

'Hello?' R. asked in a low and hesitant voice without daring to turn around.

'Yes,' replied a male voice. It was a deep and guttural voice whose words echoed against the walls. 'I'm here, right behind you.'

With a jerky movement R. turned around and discovered with horror that a man was standing in one of the corners, in the near total darkness where the flickering light did not reach. With his eyes now used to the dark R. was able to make out a tall figure in a shabby blue suit. Underneath that suit the man was wearing an almost comically creased white shirt dotted with brownish stains. Even his trousers were grossly oversized and entirely covered up the man's shoes.

'I'm pleased to make your acquaintance,' the man said with a gesture that seemed to imitate a handshake.

The gravelly sound of those words directed R.'s attention to his face. He had an extremely pale complexion with short white hair thinning at the front and cheekbones sharpened by a knife. His bright grey eyes radiated the intensity of an eagle's stare and made him appear younger than he was. Only his wrinkled skin and especially the absurdly prominent crow's feet around his eyes gave him away as an old man.

'Who are you?' R. asked hesitantly.

The man laughed so hard at that question that he shook a little and beat up his chest. R. shuddered at the explosive force of that laugh, which would have raised the hair on the heads of the walkers-by if the sound of thunder had not muffled it.

'Are you really asking me that question? But it was you who requested a meeting with me!'

During an interval of a few seconds the two men stared at each other in silence.

'What are you talking about? I haven't made any such request,' R. said, overcome with confusion. A part of him wanted to ask if this was some kind of joke but the intensity of his interlocutor made him dread a dangerous reaction, so instead he kept his mouth shut and endured another shattering roar of laughter.

'Are you sure?' the old man queried back with perverse insistence. He stared into R.'s eyes with two frozen lances so chilling that R. was struck into complete paralysis. With helpless terror R. saw the man scratch his chin pensively and slowly advance towards him, frowning like a perplexed sleuth. Within a few seconds he was facing R. at less than a meter's distance. With piercing eyes still riveted on R., his inquisitive expression morphed into a grin.

'It is you! You had me wondering for a second there,' the man exclaimed with satisfaction. 'I am an old man at this point, but my memory has remained sharper than a teenage boy's thanks to my healthy lifestyle,' he added, smiling wide with pride. 'I recognise you from the photograph on your résumé. You have been invited to an interview, haven't you? Actually, before you answer, let me show you again how good my memory is. I believe your interview is scheduled for…' and raising the palm of his bony hand he lifted four fingers.

R. was left speechless. The date gestured by the stranger was correct. Sensing that he was getting dizzy, R. tried to make a move towards the street but the old man grabbed his shoulder from behind and detained him with dreadful authority.

'Don't worry, I won't keep you for much longer,' he whispered in R.'s ear. 'I cannot force you to honour the meeting that you had requested. But I trust that you understand the consequences of this desertion. Do you confirm that you are cancelling our meeting?'

By a reflex of self-defense R. tried to free himself from the stranger's hold and push him back into his corner, but as he woke up from his stupor he realised that was only pushing into empty space. The old man with the eagle eyes had evaporated like a ghost. Had he just been hallucinating?

The almost foreign sound of a car honking brought to him back to full awareness. Only at that moment did he realise that he was standing right in the middle of the street, drenched with rain and blocking the traffic. Urged on by a mechanical impulse he ignored his state of shock and hurried to the café where Elsa was probably waiting for him, though in his haste he neglected to check his watch.

*****

The café was a recent addition to the city, so recent that it still lacked a name. It shared half of its premises with a bike shop, also new and owned by the same person. This curious combination lent the café a bizarre but not unpleasant aesthetic. The walls were covered with pictures and drawings of bikes of various colours, tyres hung from the ceiling, and various other items of gear were scattered across the space for decorative purposes. In the evening the waiters transformed the premises into a bar by rearranging the furniture around the large rectangle at the centre of the main room where the bar itself was located. Once the tables and armchairs were added to the bikes and pieces of gear, not a whole lot of room was left for the customers to move about. As a result those standing at the bar waiting to make their orders blocked the way for all but the slimmest and most agile customers.

That night was pay day, so the place was extremely crowded. R. made his way into the café, soaked and haggard-looking. At first he failed to locate Elsa through the impenetrable wall of people. The image of her sitting in the corner by the bathroom entered his mind because he hated that particular spot and hoped she had avoided causing him such pain. But at that moment another pain, that of merely trying to sustain the image of Elsa in his mind, obliterated his psychical strength. He felt too weak to even try to locate Elsa in what appeared to him like an impossible maze.

When R.'s wretched appearance began to frighten the strategically placed customers, it looked like luck was finally on his side. Most of them backed away in terror, leaving R. just enough room to manoeuvre through the crowd. A voice muted by the ambient noise seemed to ask if he was alright. As he laboriously snaked his way through, he asked himself how people who barely knew each other could have so many things to talk about. 'Alcohol and the hatred of scapegoats,' he reckoned.

Soon R. found Elsa waving at him from one of the corners. The fact that it was not the corner next to the bathroom made him breathe a long, deep sigh of relief. Already Elsa's radiant smile was all over her face and that alone helped him refocus his thoughts.

Elsa pointed to the chair to her right. By the time she withdrew her hand, R. felt like he had already been sitting on it for a while.

'You're drenched, you should go fix yourself in the bathroom with the hand drier,' she said with a frown.

Unresponsive, R. stared at her big blue eyes and long flowing hair. He lost himself for a moment in that wonderful nose of hers. On any other face that nose would have been slightly too long, but not on hers. It was a thin nose shaped in the perfect continuation of her forehead; combined with her bright eyes and slender figure, it endowed her with the profile of a mermaid.

'I'm speaking to you,' Elsa complained, patting R. softly on the shoulder. R. writhed but forced himself to nod. His heart was beating violently against his ribcage.

'I'm listening,' he answered feebly. 'I just need to adjust to the crowd and the temperature in here.'

He pointed out that his clothes were drying at quick speed. At this Elsa smiled and turned her patting into a caress.

'It's good to see you, R.,' she said. 'I'm sorry that this place is so busy, I should have anticipated that.'

R. looked at her without answering but with a serene expression. 'Let's get something to drink,' he said without prompting, and got up without waiting for an answer. With difficulty he inched his way to the bar and waved at the bartenders to catch their attention.

Who was the man with the eagle eyes? If that man really worked for R.'s future interviewers, why was he dressed in that shabby blue suit? R. lost himself in replays of their encounter. He wondered if the bleak weather combined with his vivid imagination had caused him to hallucinate, but that hypothesis did not appeal to him. A bartender with a thick black moustache came towards him and asked him if he had been served. R. shook his head but failed to utter any sound in response. It now dawned on him that he didn't know what Elsa wanted to drink.

'A spritz, please!' she shouted from behind, divining his thoughts.

With a reflexive nod R. ordered a spritz and a double whiskey for himself. It was mediocre whiskey but R. was not in the mood to weigh his options carefully.

'Have you been stressed at work lately?' Elsa asked, shaking her cocktail.

'Not particularly. It's mostly the same everyday routine,' R. said, shrugging his shoulders.

Elsa's subtle frown indicated concern, so R. felt the urge to justify himself for the gloomy expression on his face.

'There is something else. Something that has been stressing me a bit. I'm going to a job interview early next week, and it hasn't been off my mind ever since I heard the news. I don't know why I'm obsessing over it, but I am.'

Elsa looked at him with her playful, inquisitive eyes. Her genuine care for him was mixed with an innocent and spontaneous curiosity which was the source of R.'s romantic attraction to her but which sometimes seemed to overwhelm her concern. She briefly congratulated R. on passing the first stage; what she really wanted to talk about was the interview itself. Of course R. noticed this and became even more secretive as a result, a move which added fuel to the fire of Elsa's temperament and only made her ask more questions. Her attempts at poking holes into R.'s line of defense were unsuccessful because R. had prepared for their encounter and anticipated them all.

'I would rather not talk about the interview right now,' he dropped with a casualness so distant it actually sounded firm.

Elsa pouted but had to grudgingly accede to R.'s request. Imperceptibly her frustration filtered through the ensuing chat about her tourism studies, keeping it dry and surface-level just enough to frustrate R. in turn. The room was getting stuffier by the minute and now some loud rock music was coming out of the two enormous speakers at the back.

'Jesus, this is getting annoying,' R. complained with a nervous clenching of his fists. Elsa noticed the grinding of his teeth.

'Do you want to sit outside? The heaters are on,' she suggested so meekly that R., who kept looking around him distractedly, completely failed to heed her utterance. It took Elsa another attempt to succeed, but by that point she was not even sure that R. was in the mood to continue talking.

The door to the smoking area was conveniently located right next to Elsa's chair, so they were able to make their way out without running into any bothersome customer. It opened onto a calm and poorly lighted side street with a row of tables under shadows of trees. The light produced by invisible people's cigarettes and lighters provided a nice complement to the defective streetlamps.

'Over there, a free table,' Elsa said, taking R. by the hand. The icy surface of that hand hurt her in equal measure to R.'s enjoyment of the tactile interaction.

'It's so much better out here,' R. said, sitting down. Elsa nodded in silence while rubbing her hands under the table. Without a trace of shame R. asked her what they had been talking about.

'Oh yes, your studies,' he said after taking a sip of whiskey. He called her brave for her choice to go back to studying and insisted that her decision would eventually pay off. Elsa noticed that he was trying to suppress a yawn but attributed it to evening fatigue.

R. was struggling mightily to maintain his focus on Elsa's words. At that exact moment he could still not tell if the reason was his state of shock or the banality of her conversation. Elsa liked to go into excessive detail in narrating her day to day, as if the mere act of listing things helped her to exorcise her own boredom. Whether the recipient of her information was entertained only seemed a passing worry to her.

R. tried to concentrate by scrutinising her face and figure, but as a result a wave of distracting thoughts drifted in and out of his mind. How on earth could he succeed in becoming Elsa's lover? She was always talking. The fertility of her mind translated itself into large surpluses of words and sentences and required great mental agility to keep up. In her company the faintest happening in the environment could become the next topic of conversation. Let a classmate drop a comment about a hike in the mountains and Elsa would soon be found recounting her spiritual experiences in northern India; let someone complain about how long it took to be served at a bar, Elsa would retort that time is only a relative concept. Any hint of a name thrown at her had the potential to turn into an epic narrative about friendship and betrayal. None of those traits left much of an opening for a love declaration. But those were also precisely the instances that led R. to question his love for Elsa. That love seemed to come with too many bumps and hurdles; perhaps it was only infatuation.

'May I sit next to you?' asked a female voice endowed with a timbre as unfamiliar as the bark of a tree in a virgin forest. 'I can't find a seat anywhere.' Looking up, R. and Elsa lost themselves in the long shadow hovering over them.

When at last the failing lights revealed her appearance the stranger showed a forced, contorted smile. She had incredibly sharp cheekbones, but R. soon realised that the cause behind those cheekbones was not her facial structure. The woman standing in front of them was so cadaverously thin that she wouldn't have stood out in a graveyard, were it not for the scarlet red lipstick smudged all around her mouth. But the unnaturalness of her smile, combined with her covert vampirism, was not even what troubled R. the most. The menacing shade of dark blue worn by the old man had been marked into his brain and thus with a terrifying lack of effort he recognised that colour in the oversized dress the woman was wearing. For a body like hers any outfit would have been oversized, but the recurrence of that shade of blue turned R.'s blood to red ice.

'May I sit next to you, please?' the woman repeated after a brief interval of silence. With a frown she gestured her mild impatience and made her large rimless glasses stand out. Until then neither R. nor Elsa had noticed them because of the blurring half-darkness. Somehow the glasses added to the subtle refinement of her face and concealed its more repellent aspects.

'Of course you can sit with us!' Elsa cried with enthusiasm. R. nodded vaguely in approval and took another sip of whiskey. Underneath his cool exterior his heart skipped a beat.

'Thank you!' the woman said with a tone of gratitude, sitting down happily nearer to the light and revealing her ginger braids. No doubt her angular figure made her look older than she really was. R. estimated that she was in her mid-forties.

'I think I can hear an accent when you speak. Where are you charming people from?' the woman asked without the emotion required to match her question.

Elsa didn't pick up the disconnect and candidly replied that her mother was from Uruguay.

'Uruguay!' the woman cried with unexpected trepidation. 'What a coincidence! I am also from Uruguay,' she added, noticing as she replied the growing excitement on Elsa's face. 'I was born and raised there. Like you I have a foreign parent. Well, I had. My father was from

Berlin, but he died when I was very young. I hardly even remember him.'

She took out an old handkerchief and wiped her eyes under her glasses. Ever since sitting down she had not looked at R. a single time.

Now Elsa too was beginning to feel uncomfortable. In an attempt to change the course of the conversation she asked the red-haired woman if she still lived in Uruguay.

The guest greeted her words with a raucous laugh.

'Of course not! I have been a diplomat for twenty years,' she said. 'But I do get the chance to visit from time to time. Last spring I had a number of meetings to attend in Montevideo, so I allowed myself a few days off after that to pay my regards to old family members.'

As a casual aside she mentioned that one of her meetings had been with José Murica, the president of the country. 'I was invited to his farm on the outskirts of the capital and stayed for the night. You do know that old Pépé Mujica lives on a farm, yes?' she now threw at R. without warning.

As she shifted her glance towards R. her face assumed an even more alien expression. She licked her lips nervously and grabbed a glass of water which she brought to her mouth to try to hide her chattering teeth. But through the water's reflection her teeth only looked bigger and more alien, as if she had bitten into a poisonous fruit. R. masked his unease under a layer of nonchalance and answered that he knew about Pépé Mujica's farm.

'But so does everyone else in this city,' he could not resist adding with a weary shrug. All the while he was still trying to convince himself that the woman's dress was of a different shade of blue than the old man's. Perhaps his shrug had only been meant to distract her attention from that secret interest, but his lightly squinting eyes gave him away.

'You are overestimating the people of this city, young man,' the woman answered in a sinister tone. She insisted on the fact that few people in ___ knew about Mr. Mujica and that she found that fact shocking. R. agreed without conviction that he had exaggerated, but remarked in his fellow citizens' defense that Uruguay was a small country, rarely at the centre of international attention.

'It might not be a big country, but our president has a massive heart,' the woman insisted. 'He donates ninety percent of his salary to charity organisations. Did you know that?'

The tensely insistent tone of the woman was beginning to annoy R. despite his general disinterest in what she had to say. 'Why on earth is she putting me on the spot like that?' he wondered. In an attempt to redirect the course of the conversation he asked Elsa a question which he forgot about instantly.

For some arcane reason Elsa slightly reprimanded him for interrupting the woman before she had finished her point. 'Forgive my friend,' Elsa said to their guest, 'he is feeling a little on edge these days. Do continue, please.'

R. was taken aback by Elsa's defiance but he concealed his surprise by taking a sip of whiskey and reckoning internally with the strength of the Uruguayan national feeling. His reckoning, however, was interrupted by the spectacle of the woman's effusive gratitude to Elsa for allowing her to resume. She took Elsa's hand, caressed it with her crackling claws, and offered her a ghastly smile that spread yet more lipstick around her mouth.

'Thank you, my dear. I appreciate your solicitude. It really saddens me to witness how little-known Mr. Mujica is on this continent. Did I tell you that during my visit to his farm, he spent the night sleeping in the doghouse? After dinner we had only a brief chat on account of his great fatigue. Presiding a country takes a lot out of you, so I understood him and didn't feel offended. But I wasn't expecting the incredible sentence he pronounced as he stood up to collect the dishes. With a solemnity that I will never forget, he said that it had been a long time since he had let the dog sleep in his bed, and that it was time to reward the faithful little animal for being such a good companion. So he went upstairs with a bowl full of leftover chicken and placed it in his bedroom, right next to the night table, to attract the dog. You know dogs, they would never miss an opportunity like that. When Mr. Mujica came back, the dog was already upstairs enjoying his feast. But the most stupendous part of it all was the sight of Mr. Mujica going outside and proceeding on all fours to the little doghouse. His dignity was unblemished!' she cried with tears in her eyes.

Having already decided that the woman was a compulsive liar and most likely a social outcast, R. did not take her absurd story seriously. Discreetly he glanced at Elsa to gauge whether she had the same reaction. With a sigh of disappointment he recognised in Elsa's expression the sparkling enthusiasm she used to show in reaction to things that he himself said. It now looked like the stranger and her unlikely tales had been substituted for him.

Elsa thanked the woman for sharing that story, which she called 'a reason to believe in humanity', and promised to read the Wikipedia article on José Murica. After expressing the wish that she could visit Uruguay more often, she excused herself and went to the bathroom. R. somehow could not believe that he was left alone with the enigmatic woman. He wasn't frightened by the prospect, but until that moment the possibility of it had not occurred to him.

All throughout her otherworldly smile had not left her features, and she was now directing the full intensity of that smile at R. She seemed intent on hearing out loud what his thoughts were on the story. 'Come on, tell me what you really think,' her defiant eyes were saying.

R. sensed that he was getting nervous from the compulsive shaking of his knees. 'What I really think?' he answered the unasked question, but to his surprise the woman nodded in agreement. 'Well, I would lie to you if I said that I believed you. To a logical mind, your account presents a certain number of problems.'

'What problems? What problems?' the woman repeated anxiously, twisting her mouth a little.

'Well, for one,' R. continued unfazed, 'Pepe Mujica is known to be quite a stout man. Unless he owns an especially huge dog, I can't see how he would ever fit into a doghouse. You also forgot to mention his wife, First Lady Lucia Topolansky.'

'What about his wife? What about her?' the woman almost cried, her eyes getting dangerous close to the brink of their sockets.

But it was too late to contain R.'s unconscious cruelty. 'You must know that Lucia Topolansky has a notoriously strong temper. She would never agree to spend the night with a dog. That's a silly idea,' he concluded coolly.

The red-haired woman opened her mouth wide in horror.

'Entschuldigung!' she cried, unleashing a salvo of long and intricate German sentences.

R. was taken off guard. He tried to explain to the offended party that he did not understand German very well, but each one of his attempts was interrupted by another streak of foreign reprimands. In that excited maelstrom R. thought he heard some Spanish, some Greek and even a few words of Russian. Glancing around him in search of support, he located only shadows of faces dimly revealed by the light of the cigarettes.

'I see your mastery of languages is very limited, young man. How dare you doubt my words if you are not even a polyglot!' she shouted in anger.

R. let out a gasp of terror and pushed his chair back, driven by instinctive fear and the desire to escape from the deranged creature. At this the woman laughed with open contempt.

'A coward too, I see! That is certainly a side of your résumé I wasn't expecting.'

At that moment R. felt the grip of a hand on his shoulder which made him jump backwards. 'What are you standing up for?' Elsa asked. She was smiling at him with an expression of confusion mixed with candour.

'Elsa!' R. cried out of relief, falling into Elsa's embrace.

'Did she leave?' Elsa said, pointing behind him. R. turned around and noticed that the seat in front of him had been left vacant.

'You didn't scare her away, did you?' Elsa asked, but R. only saw her scowl in his mind's eye, he didn't actually listen to her words and thus made no answer. He was standing there with dangling arms, hypnotised by the empty chair. Assuming that this was only a prolongation of R.'s earlier state, Elsa got him to sit down and stroked his shoulder.

'Do you want something to drink? Your glass is empty,' she said.

'Water, please,' R. replied. Elsa nodded and went in.

'She could never understand,' he sighed. For a second he wondered if belief could trump understanding. If Elsa could not understand, would she still believe him out of devotion, would she not listen to his stories about the people in dark blue and think him insane?

At that moment R. realised that Elsa would understand him but not believe him, and so he decided keep the whole story to himself. An irresistible force drew him inward, convincing him that he was dealing with a deeply personal matter. Those two individuals had appeared out of nowhere to threaten him about the interview, and he had to figure out why.

A figure passed him by in the almost dark, asking him about the vacated chair. R. nodded to say they could take the chair and peered at it one last time before the black vortex engulfed it.

'Maybe not such a luckless thing, being engulfed,' he mused. Yet the very thought process which underlay that remark caused him to question his state of shock. He didn't really feel out of sorts anymore, were it not for a faint stomach ache. From the moment that Elsa had seized him in her arms, lacking other options, all his fears had vanished. But with it the rush of adrenaline that had accompanied them vanished, too.

Sometimes R. fantasised about doing something illegal just to revive that rush. Of course he would never have the courage for such misdemeanours, however trivial, but because he knew he was incapable of bringing them to fruition, he was able to fantasise about them without inhibitions.

R. turned back to look through the window, where he saw Elsa waiting for his glass of water at the bar. Carefully he watched the serene expression on Elsa's face, her polite exchanges with the waiter.

'If she invites me back to hers, maybe I'll walk up to her room and strangle her in cold blood,' he said with a raucous laugh that drowned out the sound of his own words.

*****

R. slept very poorly that night. Strange nightmares kept haunting his sleep, waking him up every time with a gasp of terror. The red-haired woman would appear out of nowhere with her vampire's face and a pair of blue trousers covered in blood stains. With sadistic delight she kept away from R.'s field of vision in order to locate his blind spot and critically injure him. At intervals she was helped by Milena and Mr. Axel.

In the longest of those dreams the woman was chasing R. with an axe over an endless motorway. She was very clear and insistent that she wanted to strike him just once, right in the middle of his skull. At times she almost caught up with him, getting so close that she could easily have struck his calves or even cut off one of his legs, but she would not be persuaded to do that because it contradicted her original promise.

'I'll do it like Raskolnikov in *Crime and Punishment*!' she yelled with a swollen neck, followed by a string of insults in different languages.

'What in God's name did I do to you?' R. shouted back at his aggressor with the little breath left in him.

'You questioned my story about Pépé Mujica, you called me a liar! But he did sleep in that doghouse, I saw him with my own eyes, you blithering fool!' she howled, completely possessed.

'What if I told you I believe your story now? I changed my mind,' R. pleaded, still racing forward.

'Too late! It's way too late!' the woman shouted back, and with her free hand she rummaged through her trouser pockets, taking out a rusty whistle which she blew into with authority. At the sound of the whistle two slim figures emerged from the sides of the highway. With the agility of gymnasts they joined arms to form a clothesline and prevent R. from passing through. Luckily for R. the result was a pale attempt at a clothesline which he found very easy to bypass. As he ran past the unknown figures he recognised the distorted faces of Milena and Axel, whose flashing eyes and wide, malignant smiles filled him with horror.

Without noticing it he slowed down a little, perhaps out of an unconscious desire to understand why Milena and Axel suddenly wanted him dead. But before he even had the time to open his mouth his hair was stroked by a sharp metallic object. The danger contained in that sensation utterly paralysed him with fear. He collapsed on the ground after the betrayal of his muscles. Only the eternally generous sun, bursting with yellow light, allowed him to descry three shadowy faces slowly circling around him. With callous delight they took a long time to lift their axes in the air, hissing and chuckling to themselves like wild beasts.

R. woke up in a confused and agitated state with his heart literally pounding inside his chest. Although he couldn't see himself in the mirror, his expression was even more haggard than before he had gone to bed. Weakly he reached for the glass of water on his night table to slake an unbearable thirst. After he turned the light off again he noticed something move along the opposite section of wall, right above his desk. Nervously clenching his fists under the blanket, he persuaded himself that nothing had happened and shut his eyes. But he opened them soon again in a stupor, with cold sweat spreading on his temples, when he heard an indistinct screeching noise coming from the wall.

The spectacle he witnessed sent a wave of chills down his backbone. A plastered cast of the man with the eagle eyes was crawling its way out of a hole in the wall. On each of his slowly emerging shoulders a pair of white gargoyles was perched, gazing at R. with their malicious red eyes. The old man stretched one of his arms towards R. and pointed at him in an accusatory manner.

'You are a hypocrite!' the gesture seemed to say, but it was not accompanied by sounds. R. closed his eyes for a brief moment and when he opened them again he realised that it was morning.

*****

On the tram to work R. reckoned that a holiday might not be such a bad idea after all. He felt like he was slowly descending into madness for reasons unexplained, the main symptom of which was his growing inability to distinguish facts from illusions, reality from fiction. He looked outside at the city fleeting by.

'Movement creates such much vagueness,' he thought. He linked that thought to the vagueness from which all mystery originates. Under that light the interview seemed like a talisman.

When R. arrived at the office he saw Axel busily engaged in the act of coffee making. Out of dread of what might happen after the intake R. crawled his way stealthily to his office. As R. slipped behind Axel he noticed a mark on the back of his neck. It was a small cut, thin and red, in the shape of a crescent. The mark greatly aroused R.'s curiosity. In less than a second he had conjured up different scenarios to explain the accident, none of which satisfied him. It looked like someone had attacked Axel and grazed the nape of his neck with a sharp object.

'The axe,' R. thought with a shudder. 'The red-haired woman wasn't happy with his clothesline and tried to punish him!'

There existed a simple way to determine the validity of that thesis. If it was true, then Milena must also have a mark on the back of her neck.

R. opened the door to his office and sat down at his desk, pondering. Milena had not arrived yet. What if she attempted to cover the wound with band aid? But that would only succeed in hiding the wound, not the fact that she had one. On the contrary it would draw people's attention to that fact.

R. laughed as he realised that Milena was precisely the kind of person to fool herself in that way. But quickly his mirth gave way to frustration. He didn't like having to wait to discover the truth of a matter which had somehow become highly important to him. To pass the time he checked the train times to the south of ___, having decided that his declining mental health required a visit to his family. His sparse list of emails foreshadowed a quiet day at the office; he would be able to get on an early train.

'Hello!' Milena greeted him with unusual sprightliness. R. greeted her back in a tepid tone, disappointed to see that Milena was wearing a scarf. It was impossible to say whether that scarf was used to cover a wound or as a fashion item. 'I should concentrate on my work,' R. said to himself.

The air was abnormally hot in the windowless building that morning. 'If only that scarf wasn't made of silk. Then it would be obvious that she is intentionally keeping it on,' he reasoned. His state of distraction impeded his work and as a result he made a few blunders on social media. For some reason he kept mixing up the organisation's English account with its French account, posting updates every time in the wrong language before quickly deleting them.

Out of nowhere R. experienced a pang of envy of Milena's trilingual talents. Milena noticed R.'s slightly hostile look and stared back at him inquisitively, but made no comment. Shortly after she complained about the heat and took off her scarf at last, revealing an entirely spotless neck. Although immediately relieved, R. decided that he was going insane and proceeded in haste to book his train journey back home. 'I can study for the interview while I am on the train,' he thought.

R. yawned from lack of sleep, which triggered a sequence of additional yawns.

'Maybe coming to work early isn't for you,' Milena quipped.

'I didn't come to work early,' R. casually darted back, redirecting his glance to his email box.

Soon after R. smelled the smoke oozing out of Milena's ears, but he kept his eyes fixed on his screen. He enjoyed, without knowing why, the fact that he was feeling devious that morning. Later in the day, when he stood up to grab a coffee, he asked Milena if she needed anything from the kitchen. 'Just by way of an apology,' he reflected whilst walking.

The day followed its uneventful course until the clock struck half four. By then R. had completed his social media monitoring and sloganeering for the Mali project. He had essentially nothing left to do except pretending to work for an extra half an hour and take his leave.

The thought occurred to him that he had no right to blame his colleagues for playing a game of pretense while he himself spent so much time merely pretending to work. Curiously he never pictured himself as lazy. In fact, he never felt like he had too little to do. His actual work, the work to be done to satisfy his employers, was the source of the drudgery. R. remembered Elsa's remark that time was only a relative concept, and began to feel more sympathetic towards that idea.

The powerful inertia of boredom led him back by the hand to the scenes of the day before, and he found himself growing anxious again. Suddenly changing his plans, he started searching through the staff and board sections of all the websites he could think of in the hope of identifying the two strangers in the dark blue outfits. Alas, he only found a void. Everything seemed to suggest that they didn't exist. R. wished he was suffering from a temporary state of delusion, as if confirming their nonexistence had become his obsession. Unfortunately he could not shake off the memory of Elsa's interactions with the red-haired woman. Quickly he perceived the uselessness of asking Elsa for confirmation that the meeting didn't happen. He could recall her enthusiasm with too much clarity.

'I better head off,' R. mumbled to himself after looking at the time and realising that he was about to run late. In the interval the rain had begun to pour, which he took as a sign of his right decision. When he got to the central train station he found it extremely busy.

'What a poorly designed station,' he couldn't help thinking every time he had to go there. Putting on his headphones for protection, he sped his way through the formless mass of people huddled together inside. A few minutes later he reached the platform where the familiar train was waiting until departure.

R. contemplated the enormous blue-grey shape for a while. The memory of a piece of philosophical writing he had once authored occurred to him. In that essay he had used the example of a train to illustrate a principle about propositional analysis in the philosophy of language.

'I am taking a train back to ___ today,' he kept repeating to himself. 'Such a subtly complex sentence.'

As he replayed the sentence in his mind, the vague but creeping notion that he had failed to plumb its depths began to bother him. How could he have missed the alternative analyses now vying for his attention? He wondered if infatuation with a woman had distracted him from work at the time without his noticing it. 'Quite possible,' he whispered with a sigh, 'quite possible.'

*****

During the familiar journey R. found it nearly impossible to concentrate on the interview. The cause of his confusion was the woman seated in front of him.

He thought she eerily resembled the silent lady in the tramway. She had the same elongated forehead and pale inquisitive eyes, and kept twitching her lips in a judgemental manner. R. recognised a trace of nobility in her ageing features. The only marked difference with the other lady was one of dress. The woman facing him was covered in black from head to toe and looked like she had just attended a funeral. She was staring in front of her gravely, pervaded by a sadness so translucid that R. could not tell where she was looking, and he felt very unnerved as a result of not knowing.

Every few seconds he would suddenly look away, then slowly reorient his gaze back to the woman in the hope of finding her asleep. But every time he checked the old woman was still lost in her listless gaze. It sucked all the life out of her two penetrating grey orbs. At a loss for a strategy, R. rummaged through his bag and picked up a book by Kierkegaard, *The Sickness Unto Death*, to use as a cover over his eyes while pretending to read.

That little trick felt so contrived that R. was not able to sustain it for very long. Only a minute later he dejectedly put the book away. His frustration prevented him from noticing the two little holes in the cover.

A member of the train crew stopped by them with a stall carrying food and drinks. R., who was dying to find something to do with his shaking hands, asked for a cup of decaffeinated coffee.

'With pleasure,' the anonymous crew member replied with surprising enthusiasm. The man appeared thrilled by such a fresh and unusual occurrence. With exquisite delicacy he poured the coffee into a little cardboard cup and placed it on the table in front of R. The lady opposite was not asked if she wanted a drink or a snack. She hardly paid attention to those goings on.

R. almost burned the tip of his fingers trying to take the cup into his hands. With a muted gasp of pain he put the cup back on the table and looked at it helplessly. At that point a strange occurrence took place. The lady in black was no longer staring into the distance but at the scalding cup of coffee. She seemed especially mesmerised by the steam coming out of it. R. observed her fixated features for a while. The protruding veins on her temples were forming little rivulets of purple all the way to the sides of her eyes. Her motionlessness made R. wonder for a second if she had just had a stroke, but with restored concentration he detected some very faint bodily movements around her hands. Those were as pale as her face, but more wrinkled, with long and fine fingers akin to those of a pianist.

'Why is she so interested in the cup?' R. asked himself in wonderment. Then he recalled that the tramway woman always hopped off at the same city stop to disappear around a corner where R. pictured a seedy coffee shop located between two faceless apartment complexes. In his mind's eye the buildings looked virtually the same as the one where the man with the eagle eyes had ambushed him. A dirty entrance hall with cigarette butts strewn across the floor was lit by a flickering light reflected in the green glass of broken bottles. R. noticed a little pearl of saliva foaming around a corner of the woman's mouth. He toyed with the idea of just giving her his coffee but eventually changed his mind. He didn't know her; in fact he didn't even know if she even wanted to drink coffee.

Overwhelmed by indecision once again, R. witnessed his hands move by themselves towards the cup. At the touch of the cup his fingers did not burn but rather sent him a pleasant tingly sensation. It was now time to drink, so R. licked his lips in anticipation. Instinctively he looked around him one last time. When his glance crossed the old lady's he noticed that she was now smiling wide at him. He watched in astonishment her crooked but perfectly white teeth offering themselves to him, behind which a concealed voice seemed to entreat him: 'Come on, drink from the cup! I want to see you drink from the little cup!' So without thinking R. took a sip, which tasted fine, and the expression on the old lady's face slowly shifted from curiosity to rapture.

She was now demanding that R. take more sips. R. followed suit without knowing why he was being so docile, and that seemed to fill the old lady with a sense of heavenly ecstasy more intense than the first taste of love. The transaction continued until R. realised there was nothing left to be savoured.

'I finished it,' he said to the woman, looking up.

'I know,' she answered with tender smile. 'I just saw the look of disappointment growing on your face.'

At these words R. straightened himself up in self-defense. 'I didn't feel that inside,' he said, shaking his head.

At that moment the old woman seized R.'s empty hand and caressed it softly. 'It was the contrast, young man. The contrast in your expression before and after you finished your coffee. I don't think you have any idea of how much you enjoyed that cup. Your delight was so contagious that I almost wished I had been in your place. Happiness is a rare thing on the faces of youth,' she observed, looking out the window with pensive eyes.

Now that the old lady was talking, R. realised that he found her presence calming. Her voice was soft and enveloping, full of kindness and wisdom. He asked her if they had met before. She answered that she could not remember.

'I was only in ___ for a few days to visit my daughter. I retired a few years ago,' she added in a faint tone of nostalgia.

R. asked her what had been her occupation.

'Psychologist,' the lady answered. 'Something like that, anyway. I specialised in reading emotions off people's faces. This is why your case was so immediately interesting to me. You seem so extremely conflicted, like there is a constant war raging inside you.'

At this R.'s heart skipped a beat, but externally all he showed was an air of skepticism. 'She is already making so many assumptions about me,' he thought. 'I should try to stay on my guard, although she seems nice.'

The spreading silence made his unease more acute and once again the only solution he found was words. 'I'm not sure it's a good idea to make guesses and then turn them into truth,' he objected. 'If we have never met before, you cannot pretend to know me, psychologist or not.'

Only after he had given that retort did he realise the retort had cost him some psychic energy. It was always his body rather than his mind that liked to remind him of his aversion to conflict. To calm his trembling bones he quickly shifted his glance to the landscape outside. Some distant patches of bright lavender fields could be seen blending with the rolling hills of the south under a smiling sun. The train was already getting close to its destination. R. was astounded by the shortness of the trip.

The old woman looked at him with her large, benevolent eyes. R. thought he could see a hint of sorrow in them, though he would not have dared to ponder its deep recesses. It was probably forever locked up in the silent libraries of the past, which would remain as inaccessible to him as the ancient library of Alexandria. But that did not matter because the old lady was carrying those memories in her sentences and facial expressions, even in her hand gestures. Everything about her seemed shrouded in the veil of a long lost era, an era where nobility and grace were the most prized of the virtues.

R. felt her hand pressing his hand once again. 'I would never claim to know your life, young man. But I can see with my own eyes what you radiate right now in this train. And what I see is a great deal of anguish. You seem to be lost in a sea of uncertainty. Which is why I would like you to let me… help you,' she said softly, almost in a murmur. There was a hint of supplication in her voice.

'But why would you want to help me, even supposing that I needed help?' R. asked candidly.

At this the lady smiled again, but it was a sad smile. 'It's a long story,' she said.

Intrigued, R. insisted that he had nothing to do until the train's arrival in ___ and that he was happy to hear her story.

The old lady took out a tissue from her handbag and placed it on the table. With that gesture she seemed to anticipate the possibility of tears, though her expression remained serene. However, serenity did not survive on her features for very long before it gave way to sadness. It wasn't just a generic kind of sadness, but the specific sadness of grief that was now invading her face. Her lips quivered a little as she pressed R.'s hand ever more firmly.

'I had a son once,' she said, her eyes still fixed on R. 'He was my eldest child. A bright and beautiful boy with inquiring blue eyes and a golden head of hair, always a little unruly around the sides… My husband and I tried to raise him with all the love that we could give him. We always had to cope with the fact our son was a little different from the other young boys. He didn't seem interested in the real world. He was always dreaming. As he grew older he turned out to be highly gifted. As a result he always did extremely well in school, but ever so slowly I sensed in him a distance, almost like a renunciation in the face of life. When he was very young he would be clumsy and awkward, but loving. By the time he became a teenager, he was no longer showing his family any affection. He was not unpleasant or cruel, not at all, he was always very polite and well-mannered, but he just no longer seemed concerned by what was going on around him. I know that I am not explaining myself very well. But this is because my son's increasingly alien attitude has always been so hard to explain, even to this day. As his parents we still loved him, and took it as our duty to provide for his future. The problem is that over time, my son and my husband grew dangerously used to being estranged from each other.'

She explained that her husband had recently passed away from a long illness that she would rather not recall. He had worked in the department of logistics of a large corporation, but seemed to have harboured the constant regret of not pursuing a career in mathematics. The estrangement caused by the son's moodiness gradually became a focus of the father's obsessions, to the extent that he began to neglect the education of their daughter. R. insisted on remaining silent while the lady spoke, but he presumed that the daughter mentioned was the one the old lady had recently visited in ___ .

But then, as the woman resumed her narrative, R. became aware of a renewed sense of unease growing inside him. Because his interlocutor was focused on telling her story, he was able to branch out unnoticed into other preoccupations that began to populate his mind. Why was he there, passively acquiescing in the wallowing delusions of a stranger? He was moved by her, though he couldn't quite say why. The fact that her face reminded him of the tramway lady did not suffice to explain his emotion. There was something else, though he couldn't put his finger on it, and his inability to put a name on the origin of his interest bothered him.

Without warning he raised his hand, and this had the desired effect. The old lady stopped her narration mid-sentence but her face was unable to conceal her perplexity. For a second she stared at R. open-mouthed.

'I can already tell what the conclusion of your story is going to be, madam,' he said. 'Your husband had always wanted to be a mathematician, and your son was gifted, therefore your husband projected onto your son the desire to be a mathematician. But your son didn't want any of that, and because he was smart he was even able to sense the projection. No wonder that by that point he was completely discouraged from the idea of studying mathematics. But that didn't pacify your husband, so I imagine a lot of strong words must have been exchanged between them at the time. I feel sorry for your son, he shouldn't have been subjected to his father's resentment.'

The warmth in the lady's eyes had turned to freezing cold.

'My son is dead,' she said. 'He broke off from our family after finishing secondary school and volunteered to work in a hospital in Palestine. A few weeks later he was dead. The Israeli forces bombed the hospital and the ceiling collapsed on his head. He was crushed so brutally that nobody could recognise his corpse,' she added in a voice smothered with tears.

The thick, heavy tears kept flowing from her eyes with such persistence that the lone tissue on the table was not enough to wipe them away, so she had to take many more tissues out of her handbag. R. had not expected the conclusion of her story to be so grim. He felt sad for her but also nervous, because he had no idea how to console the poor woman.

A light illuminated his dark, deep blue yes. A smile visiting from a faraway place gradually sketched itself on his face. R. waited until the old lady had finished drying her tears before taking her hand again. He stroked it tenderly. The woman noticed that R. was still intently looking at her but could not utter anything in return nor even stare back at him. For what seemed like a long time the two of them remained silent and motionless, facing each other like statues.

The train was now five minutes away from its destination. The woman closed her eyes to allow them to rest a little. When she opened them again, R. was gone. The train had arrived. On the table next to the empty cup, R. had left a handwritten note as a token of farewell. The old lady took the note in her hands and let herself be absorbed by its content. She smiled, but the unusual shape of her smile evoked suppressed dismay. 'I wanted to teach him something,' she thought, 'but now it is too late. He will have to fend for himself.'

*****

Alone by the pool next to a tall pine tree, his feet dipped in the cold water of autumn, R. was looking contemplatively at the pitch black sky overarching his mother's house. The stars had vanished just before his arrival, it seemed, a fact which he took with a sense of irony. But the same blackness allowed him to concentrate on the memories now drifting through his mind rendered creative by fatigue. He remembered the evenings spent chatting under the celestial vault with his father, trying to reproduce in words the wildly various shapes of the constellations. In the black void above him he was still able to intuit the peculiar symmetry of Orion and the blazing blue flames of Vega, the star that could always be found by looking directly above your head.

Once, R.'s father had told him about a distant star so massive that it could easily contain entire galaxies within itself. R. never forgot about that wonderful anecdote out of the wish to continue believing in its truth. He remembered the star's name, too, but kept it stubbornly to himself like a gemstone. The mere act of thinking about those days brought him back in time and made him feel younger. He wondered why human beings so often dreamt of creating time machines since they already had their memories.

R. pictured his father with the thick black moustache he had sported back then. He also recalled how his father would make a point of answering all his questions, even the most far-fetched, just to see happiness shine on his son's face. A boy is always looking for secret reasons to be proud of his father. Among the laws of nature, this is perhaps the one least advertised, but this doesn't take anything away from its truth. The potent truth of it buries it in the unconscious, where it remains hidden from the outside world, while the actions of the repressor continue to be drenched in it. The young R. had admired his father for many reasons, but none of them was stronger and more lasting that his father's deep, almost arcane knowledge of the sky.

But on that chilly October night R.'s father was as absent from the premises as the stars. The reason for this was no accident, but two divorces. He owned a house close to the city centre, a fifteen-minute drive away. A very short distance compared to the emotional distance which, over time, had driven the two men apart. It was hard to think of a bridge to span that crevice because the size of the opening had never been measured, yet continued to widen. It didn't help that R.'s father had little notion that this was going on. He was a busy man and not very equipped at reading people.

R. shifted his attention to more positive thoughts to calm the anxiety mounting inside his heart. He tried to focus on the hopeful feelings that had motivated his last-minute visit to the homeland. But the blackness of the sky offered him up to a void that was slowly sucking him in and within the nothingness of which all that was left to think about was his relationship with his father.

'How frustrating,' he muttered under his breath. Lowering his head to look at the blurred shape of his feet, he tried to figure out if the image stirring his imagination was from a past era of painting. In that new attempt at deflection he was once again unsuccessful. Numbed with cold, his legs tapered off into sharp but irregular little spears. At that moment he felt something rub softly against his back.

'Chestnut!' R. cried with joy at the sight of the beloved family cat, who liked to play outside on the terrace during the autumn night.

It could hardly be fathomed how attached R. was to the tiger-striped, resourceful little Chestnut. The knowledge of her fifteen years vanished at the sight of her nimble alertness and outdoor escapades. R. gave his cat a head rub. She purred loudly and bumped her little head repeatedly against the back of his hand.

'Roaming so near the edge of the pool and yet unafraid,' R. reflected with admiration. Between the opposite poles of friendliness and fierceness he saw the wanderings that animated Chestnut's life and kept her young. Deep inside he dreamt of emulating that balance, but he felt he had first to solve the puzzle that he was to himself.

R. took Chestnut in his lap and kissed the top of her head several times before he let her go explore the other parts of the garden. Following her with his eyes for a moment he saw her proud face, always held upwards, fade slowly into the darkness of the surroundings.

All throughout that time he had kept at the back of his mind the encounter with the old lady in the train. So she had wanted to help him. Help him in what way? In his opinion R. was taking care of himself quite alright, and that observation was sanctified in his mind by the recent news of the interview. What better proof that he had retained control over his life?

But then, with the force of a natural law, the peculiar cast of his spirit took hold of him again and he began to envision possible counter-evidence to his original conclusions. It could not be denied, for example, that his romantic life was a shipwreck. He had only the vaguest of ideas of the last time he had made love to a woman. R. struggled intensely to reminisce what the act of sex had felt like, but the sparse pieces of data he was able to snatch from his memory were hopelessly faint. 'At least I have never allowed myself to become a misogynist,' he thought with some satisfaction.

Suddenly the image of the red-haired woman imprinted itself on his psyche and glued itself to it. R. wondered why that image had cropped up since he found that woman physically repulsive, but soon he realised that the cause was a separate worry. She and the old man with the eagle eyes had appeared to him from within the enclosure of a nightmare and threatened him openly about the interview. They said or at least implied that they were going to fail him, and the fear of failure was so strong in R. that it overshadowed his more rational side.

Those encounters had seemed so ethereal that R. found no way of fixing his mind on them for any length of time. They sent through his body a sensation that was almost impossible to describe but which he had felt acutely when the man with the eagle eyes had seized his arm to detain him. Simultaneously the fitful and uncertain nature of that sensation struck him with the intangible blow of a vivid dream. In the haze that permeated those events there still subsisted a fragment of entertaining value, a conviction that what had happened was nothing short of extraordinary, although its implications at that point remained shrouded in mystery.

R.'s mother appeared on the terrace and asked him if he wanted to drink tea. R. nodded without knowing why. The C. family never drank tea. Yet the sheer unusualness of the occurrence attracted him and made him envision a momentous exchange with his mother.

'Let's go sit on the other side of the house,' he said. His mother nodded in silence and went back inside. R. lifted his legs out of the water, shook them a bit to regain his sensations, and got up to follow suit. Instead of going through the house he skirted it by the little path on the side which overlooked the street and connected the two terraces. A weak wind was shaking the bamboo stems dotting his path. As he walked up the stairs past the gate to the interior garden he nearly slipped in a dying puddle. Despite the reigning silence the way seemed rougher and more hostile than usual. At last R. took a left turn and saw the little marble table where his mother was sitting with the teapot and two cups oozing steam under a dim, flickering light.

R. was secretly amused by that sight because it showed a kind of initiative he was not used to seeing in his mother. 'Is it peppermint tea you made?' he asked as he sat down.

His mother nodded with a smile. 'It's better in the evening,' she said.

The two of them sipped their tea in silence for a while. The mother's unease exceeded that of her son and urged her to speak first. With a weak voice depleted by anxiety she asked him if work was going well.

R. frowned and said that his organisation had never been a paradise of excitement. 'You already knew that,' he added.

'How is Axel doing?' she asked, fondly remembering having met the man at a reception in ___ .

'The same as always,' R. said. 'He hasn't changed since that time when you met him. Always in the mood for a good joke.'

The conversation went on for a while on a light note which contrasted with the eeriness of the atmosphere. The weak light of the lamp illuminated the face of R.'s mother with an orange glow. R. could recognise her blonde curls, her sad blue eyes turned grey by the years, her distinguished traits unaffected by the growing maze of wrinkles. He remembered how beautiful his mother had been when she was young. No doubt the pretenders were starting to dwindle in number.

There is no greater tragedy than that of the human body. What becomes repellent with the passing of time remains in full view, whereas what becomes wiser and nobler has few chances of being noticed because it lies inward. Unlike the soul the body decays over time, yet oddly is the one tasked with keeping up appearances.

Elegance was not the only ageless trait that his R.'s mother had preserved. Her eyes still looked sad and pre-occupied even when she was laughing.

'Is something the matter?' R. asked.

His mother's sad eyes looked up and blinked a few times. 'I was wondering how your interview went,' she said at last, looking away. There was unmistakable, faceless pain in the tone of her voice.

'It hasn't happened yet,' R. answered coolly. 'Didn't I tell you this over the phone?'

The tacit harshness of that response stung his mother and pushed her back into silence. R. did not notice that change in attitude at first; he had already launched into a defense of his right to keep things private. As she submitted to that flood of words R.'s mother began to look worried, then puzzled. Initially R. had felt satisfied with his tirade, but the sight of his perplexed mother made him feel undermined and reignited his annoyance. He asked her if she thought he was being unfair but didn't leave her time to reply, insisting instead on the purity of his intentions.

'I'm not trying to upset you, mother, but I had to tell you this to give you a better sense of where I'm coming from. I wanted to put my angry reaction in context, because otherwise you would have thought I was gratuitously assaulting you. I don't want to talk about the interview. It is a matter of principle. Nobody is forcing me to remain silent on the matter, if this is what you're worried about.'

But R.'s mother didn't react. Instead she continued to look at him with a mixture of bafflement and concern, which did nothing to soothe his nerves. The extreme temptation to lash out at her again was only repressed by his love. It was strange that his mother's care, her sincere desire to know about the interview, should be what angered him the most. In adult life, the most vocal sons and daughters are those who regret their parents' lack of attention. Ms. C. had her own idea of the origin of R.'s hatred of encouragement and support, but she kept it to herself because it was only an intuition, and the chances were that R. would snap at her for merely flagging it.

In any case she would never change because she could not change. That inability for change was both physical and mental. She loved him too deeply; that was the simple, unalterable truth of her existence, although that love had smothered her sons and made her partners run away one after the next. In fact, K.'s case was even more extreme and belonged to a whole other dimension.

'As usual, you are overthinking things,' R.'s mother said at last.

She did not say much more than that, not just because she thought she didn't have to, but because she couldn't. That was a mistake on her part, actually; a mistake in judgement. Her love had the side effect of making her exaggerate how alike she and her son were; while in fact there was no better way of getting a message across to R. than by dressing an emotional core in rational clothing. But rational thinking was not her strong suit and in that respect at least she was not at all like R.

If she had been able to voice her intuitions properly, she would have said that people were too worried about their own lives to even think of betraying R.'s secret about the interview. She would have observed that R. was building his reality from his projections, which was the surest path to ending up alone and depressed.

'Do not cut yourself off from people just because you think your secret might be revealed,' she almost said, but she was too scared of mentioning the interview again. Instead what she actually said—because she had to actu ally say something, she thought—was worse than anything else could have been. She told her son a romantic relationship would bring him a lot of stability, and asked him if he was seeing anyone at the moment.

With flashing eyes R. listened to his mother's nocturnal advice without moving an inch. His facial expression remained still as a stone, all human warmth having departed from it. But under the table R.'s legs were shaking so violently that only the persistent banging of doors caused by the wind's blowing blocked the noise from his mother's ears. Luckily for him, all she could see was his eyes staring at her with a hostility that was difficult to place. The foreign aura of that hostility had its centre in R.'s not even bothering to reply to her question. With meekness she received the signal that she had been trespassing and looked down at her cup for a while. She regretted the bad timing of her question, though she didn't regret the question itself.

R. took a sip of herbal tea to clear his throat. 'I understand what you are trying to say to me, mother,' he said. 'And I know that you want the best for me. But I think you are betraying a lack of judgement on two fronts. The first is that I am not you. I am myself. You don't always seem to have that in mind when you give me advice. The second is that, well, I am different. I am not like the others. Which means that you can't base all your expectations on my leading a normal life, because that won't happen. It will never happen, mother.'

'But are you happy?' his mother asked him suddenly, still wearing the same expression of concern.

'I don't know, what does that mean anyway?' R. answered, shrugging his shoulders. 'I honestly can't tell you if I'm happy. I would rather be honest with you than lie. Maybe I'll be happy when I become a writer, or when I find a wife. Maybe I'll be happy for the rest of my life if I hear the news that I passed the interview. Maybe I've never been happy; or maybe I've always been. Who can tell?'

A flash of hope shone briefly in his mother's irises. 'So you think that the interview…?'

'Of course I do,' R. almost shouted, irritated by the content of the question. 'But you know that I'm superstitious. Victory is not yet in sight. When the final decision has been made I will let you know, mother. But not before that.'

'Please don't take this the wrong way,' his mother answered after an interval of silence, taking her son's hand. 'A mother's nature is to worry about her children. I just want to know you're happy.'

R. interpreted his mother's insistence as a provocation. 'I'm not sure this makes sense since for all you know I might be dead tomorrow,' he darted back at her.

His mother made a face and begged him not to blackmail her. But by that point R. felt slighted and he could not physically resist the impulse to sustain his counterattack.

'It's also a bit rich coming from you. You pretend that you 'worry' about me. But where was your worry gone when father was beating me up? I won't forget those times when you turned a blind eye and slipped out of the house like a coward, not once, not twice, but hundreds of times. It was your work, the legacy you left to your children, mother. If you think that I'm not normal, you better ask yourself some questions. I am the person you're seeing now. Get used to it.'

R.'s mother was still looking down at her cup of herbal tea. She was not crying but only a blind man would have failed to see how affected she was by her son's words. Chestnut's swift little body emerged from the darkness and began to circle around the table excitedly. The cat meowed loudly and directed her yellow eyes towards the kitchen.

'She's hungry,' R.'s mother said, getting up to let the cat inside. She didn't return to the table but instead leant against the entrance door with her arms crossed. 'My son,' she said with unexpected composure, 'you always refer to that story when you want to hurt me. We've been over it a dozen times and I don't think you're being very fair.'

'Don't you dare call it a *story* when you know full well it's the truth!' R. shrieked, completely beside himself. 'You were fully complicit in what I had to endure and I will never forgive you for it. Do you understand? I will never forgive you,' he repeated, banging his fist on the table.

For a second his mother disappeared from his field of vision. This happened so quickly that R. wondered if the whole time he hadn't been talking to a shadow while the real Ms. C was in the kitchen feeding Chestnut. But shortly after she reappeared, or rather her sobbing made itself heard. It was quiet sobbing with lowered head; the subdued light had blended the colour of her hair with that of the door. Like her hair, her pain had also been covered by layers of darkness.

Suddenly attacked by a feeling of great urgency, R. got up and ran to his mother. 'I'm sorry,' he said, taking her in his arms and caressing her hair. 'I went too far, I'm sorry.'

'How can you not see the love that I have for you,' she said, struggling through her sobs. 'You are my pride and joy, R.'

'I know, I know,' he whispered. 'Sometimes I just get carried away and I lose my temper. Just like father.'

'Don't compare yourself to him,' she implored him. 'You are not like your father.'

Falling into a sullen silence, R continued to stroke his mother's hair and drifted into deep thoughts. He was saddened by the realisation that his heart disagreed with his mother's words. No matter what she might say, and no matter what he himself would say in response, he still felt like his father's son and saw no way out of inheriting the bad traits together with the good. He might try to convince himself that he was different, insist on all the peculiar quirks that made him a unique and incomparable being, but at the end of the tunnel there would only be one person ready to wait for him. It was his father.

'Every time that I find a way out, he reappears in a different form,' he murmured into his mother's ear. 'I have tried for years to get rid of him, but I fail every time. He always returns. I'm lost, mother. I don't know what to do.'

'There is one thing that you should do,' his mother said. 'I've been afraid of telling you this for a long time because I know the way you react to things. You need to talk about what happened with your father. Tell him you have not forgotten. But more not anything else, tell him how you feel and see how he reacts. You would be sur-prised how people react to things, sometimes. It might not be what you expect.'

R. shook his head and insisted sternly that he didn't see the point of addressing the past with his father.

'Consider it, please,' his mother beseeched him.

'I will consider it,' R. said, no longer knowing if he was being sincere or just compassionate. 'I just need to feel ready. And it isn't an easy thing to feel.'

Ms. C. looked up at her son and smiled at him a smile full of motherly concern. The darkness didn't reveal how R. chose to interpret that smile. But a few seconds later the thought occurred to him that the looming interview was perhaps the sign of his readiness. That realisation made him smile back at his mother, though she couldn't have known the origin of his atypical gesture.

'It's getting late,' she said. 'Help me put away the cups and the teapot, it's time to go to sleep.'

*****

R. struggled a great deal with falling asleep that night. Lying on his bed like a man on the cross, he was staring blankly at the ceiling. Intrusive thoughts were taking his mind hostage and he all he could do was witness that process. Whenever he managed to remove a thought it soon came back, followed by another, then another, until every intruder had crept its way back in. Worse, this aggressive dance of ideas produced other ideas not present at the start, which took the form of imagined defenses against the original intruders. R. came to wonder, in the midst of this vain fight against himself, how absurd it was that a hyperactive mind like his had been incapable of producing a work of genuine philosophical value, nor even a short story that at least one reader had found moving. What was the point of that surplus of intellectual energy if its only effects were corrosive? When a mind is like acid the destructive abilities end up dominating the constructive ones by dissolving them.

He was under no illusion that his behaviour towards his mother had been unjust and cruel. She was right: his intent had only been to inflict pain. The words he had spoken were not exactly the by-products of a hot-blooded disposition; that, in fact, was much more akin to his father's temperament. In his father's acts of violence there was nothing else than a temporary loss of self-control—a tilting over into madness devoid of any meaning beyond the urge to express itself quickly and explosively. On paper, it was possible to rationalise away those actions as external symptoms of instability, which pointed to a possible separation of the person targeted from the pain inflicted. 'What did I do to deserve this?' was, on the surface, not a permissible question to ask, because the violence did not target an 'I'. It was blind.

R. had rational access to those psychological strategies but what he lacked was the emotional access. For that he had no key, and yet it was what he needed most. As a result the guilt, desperately in search of a reason that would not show itself, continued to grow in the background of the everyday. It was immune to worldly success, to the ecstasies of love, even to sleep. How tragic it is that guilt should be one of the things people are most averse to opening up about, when it is so obvious that it can only be healed that way. We would notice in the mirrors that people offer us that the guilt we feel is not reflected back. But instead we shamefully keep our guilt to ourselves because we think that keeping it carefully locked in a dark room of our soul with no means of sustenance will eventually starve it to death. This overlooks the fact that guilt is precisely the kind of creature that has no need of nourishment to keep on growing. It delights in having nothing else to do than contemplate itself in its self-hatred until a larger room is needed to keep it locked away. But by then our whole soul needs to be mobilised, which means that it also becomes exposed to the appetite of its prisoner. A man with a black heart is often a man devoured by guilt.

Could a wrong reason be better than no reason at all, if the victim found a way of believing it? Is it more calming to the victim's psyche to have in front of them an event, a fact to identify as the trigger to violent behaviour, no matter how fictitious? Perhaps the flesh that is flogged, if it can somehow make sense of the flogging as a true punishment, can allow the psyche to replenish itself. In such a case the sufferer can say: 'I was flogged for that reason.' The reason may be imaginary and unjust, it doesn't matter: the psyche will find the vital resources to rebuild itself. The dim shadow of a reason will always be there to guide it out of the labyrinth. If the reason is just, the psyche will proceed in silent penitence; if it is unjust, all the psyche will have to do is follow the path symmetrically opposite to the one suggested. All that is necessary is a meaning—any meaning— to the violence. Given this, what can a man do when he is not offered that meaning? Nothing, except witness within himself the slow spread of the venom of guilt.

R. found it cruelly ironic, perhaps even a proof of God's nonexistence, that both the abuser and the victim should experience guilt. The former experiences it externally, while the latter internalises it. So from the beginning the victim's guilt has the resources to resist longer. It seemed to R. that his father had made the luckier draw.

For a moment he pondered his mother's words again and tried to enrich the picture of his own anger to highlight the difference from his father's. The main line of separation was that R. always had a reason for losing his temper. But since he knew those reasons he also felt compelled to hide them from others, because they were all connected to his guilt. Guilt was the underground cause of his barbed responses to questions asked without ulterior motive. Those questions pricked him sorely because they scratched the surface of his guilt. And how it maddened him to be able to identify that guilt as the cause, but never the psychological pathways leading from the sound of an utterance to the sensation of burning and the need for retribution!

Maybe there were no pathways but instead the utterances, like long and sharp spears dipped in poison, struck at his heart directly with a swift blow. In his darkest daydreams R. saw himself as a man born without skin, like the statue of Saint Bartholomew that haunted the Milan Duomo. With a psychic constitution made of nerves and muscles, but no skin to cover them up, who can be expected to live a peaceful life? If you touch the arm of a skinned man, even if you stroke it softly with your index finger for the fraction of a second, you will hit him with excruciating pain, and the chances are he will hit back in self-defense. But something is left unsaid here. A skinned man would never be touched by anyone, except with the intent to torture him. Things stood differently with R. because nobody could see that he was skinned. He concealed that fact to conceal his guilt.

*****

R. got up early in the morning and went to the beach. He was suddenly feeling an urge to walk in the sand and inhale the fresh marine air. The mistral wind was blowing, softly rustling the leaves of palm trees. R. strode along a large avenue bordered by two rows of expensive houses owned by absentee millionaires which gave a view of the horizon, sliced horizontally by a shimmering sheet of deep blue.

It is the easiest thing for a dreamy man to lose himself in contemplation of the sea. Its boundlessness offers the soul a vision of freedom from the enclosures of everyday life. In the city where R. worked, the rich could at least benefit from the objective reality of Lake ___'s imprisonment by the surrounding earth, which did not allow the eye to wander but forced it instead to look at their houses. A piece of rocky ground, a lonely creek covered at its rear by a miniature forest would be sooner or later revealed to belong to some retired football player. As a result the little world of wealth formed a tight circle around the lake and gave the impression of secretly possessing it. A similar scenario was unthinkable in the case of the sea, which is why R. enjoyed the sight so much.

With trembling feet sinking in the white sand where they found a warm refuge, R. crouched down and dipped his hands in the water. It was so cold that when he pulled his hands out his fingers felt numb. The heads of a few swimmers could be seen sticking out with shivering necks. There were a few families dotting the long swath of sand beach that skirted the sea all the way to the harbour, whose presence could be guessed from the boats cruising in the distance. At a leisurely pace R. followed the sand path in the direction of the harbour, delighting in the deserted atmosphere. The whole environment was like a magic spell clearing up even the most opaque of his thoughts.

R. pulled up at the sight of a figure lying in the sand right at the spot where the waves were crashing and breaking into froth. 'One of those homeless people dried up by last night's drinking,' he thought. As he moved closer the figure sat up, cupped some water with its hands and sprinkled its face with it. He was a young man with blonde curly hair, a tanned face with strong features, and strikingly broad shoulders. His clothes, a pair of blue chinos and a white shirt, were wet but smart underneath the wrinkles. He was definitely not a vagabond. The growing noise of R.'s footsteps drew the attention of the young man, who turned around to look at him with his confident, hazel eyes.

It was only when the stranger smiled at him that R. recognised who he was. 'K., it's you!' R. cried. The sheer feeling of surprise sent a lightning bolt down his spine. His brother was smiling and waving at him with his trademark candour. Though the event was not extraordinary in itself, R. still experienced it as a shock and took a while to recover from it.

'What are you doing here?' R. asked as he resumed his walk towards K.

'I hate how busy the city gets at the weekend,' K. answered with an hand gesture expressing annoyance. 'Mother told me you were visiting, so I decided to come your way.'

K. insisted that he had not meant to surprise his brother and that their encounter on the beach was totally fortuitous. R. found those words difficult to believe but he did not bother to inquire further. Without prompting, K. explained that his teaching hours that semester had been so chaotic that they were messing up his sleep pattern, so that he often woke up early on Saturday mornings. By that point R. was already pretending to listen to a topic he had no further interest in.

'I wanted to surprise you, by I guess mother couldn't resist telling you that I was visiting,' R. said, sighing.

K. laughed and reminded him that he disliked surprises anyway. They gave each other a warm, brotherly hug. 'We have a lot to catch up on,' K. said. 'But first let's try to find a café or a bar. I'm dying of thirst.'

However, R. did not look excited by the prospect of leaving the beach so soon.

'I told you I was dying of thirst,' K. insisted.

In response R. stared pensively at the horizon. 'I know, but I was hoping to spend a little more time here. I need to think.'

K. saw that his brother now seemed preoccupied but his ability for empathy was being thwarted by his thirst. 'So you don't want to catch up?' he asked.

At the sound of those words R. felt a jolt coursing through his body. He looked back at K. with eyes wide open.

'Of course I do! But first I need to clear up some thoughts I've been having. I won't be long.'

K. concealed his perplexity with another laugh, observed that R. was just being his old indecisive self, and gestured that he was about to leave. 'I'll go ahead, you can just catch up with me with your long legs,' he said. And he went on his way before R. had had the chance to respond.

'Indecisive,' R. grumbled as he followed his brother's shadow until it began to faint in the distance. Somehow the fact of his indecision being thrown at his face made him feel unjustly treated. His frustration was increased tenfold by K.'s immediate departure because it showed that K. did not believe that R. could justify himself. Instead R. was forever to be labelled an indecisive man because he had expressed the wish to take his time.

'Nonsense,' R. grumbled again. Then he shook his head as if to dispel his angry reaction. 'No, I understand why I give that impression. But it doesn't come from any weakness of spirit, and that's what I must remind K. of when I catch up with him. I can't let him get away with an impression of me that belongs to the past.'

To come up with a satisfying retort he had to be prepared. He knew what he wanted to convey about his new sense of self and the legitimacy given to the change by the news of the interview, but he had to find a way of articulating those notions properly. He focused his eyes on the reflection of the sunbeams in the crystalline surface of the waves. Those waves reminded him of all the options that his mind had access to at any given moment. Together they formed a whole map whose diverse regions, like exotic foreign destinations, all looked equally attractive. R.'s mind envisioned not any isolated location but the map that contained all the locations at once. Once the map was created it became impossible to focus on anything else than the map itself. To R. this was not indecision because he never had to hesitate between two or more options. By then he was no longer able to see the options at all. What looked like indecision was only his effort to zoom in on the map, to set his perceptive apparatus at a more granular level, in the same way that zooming in on the map of France would reveal the details of towns, roads and countryside areas.

Sensing a surge of confidence rising within him, R. turned around and tried to locate K.'s shadow. But the possibility of that shadow was blurred by the many bars and shops along the main street. Most of those establishments derived the bulk of their income from tourism, which was in full flow in the summer months but quickly died down in the early weeks of September. R. found it shocking to witness with the freshness of a visitor's glance the scenes of utter desolation scattered in front of him.

'Wait, don't walk so quickly!' R. shouted vaguely into the distance in the hope that his brother might hear him. Normally he was quite a fast walker but the situation at that moment was different because of the warm sensation that contact with the sand was giving to his feet. His mind may command his feet to walk faster but the feet would not listen. When at last he reached the hard cement of the street, R. regained full control of his body and eventually caught up with his brother.

Further down the road they had to go through a little park spread across a section of the beach in the shape of a tiny peninsula. Hedged in on one side by the sand strip and on the other by the street, the park boasted a carousel, a beach volleyball sand court and an ice cream shop. It was a fixture of the town, and unlike the other spots it never seemed to suffer the exodus of the post-summer months.

R. was struck by how laid back the parents were in that park. They barely seemed be keeping watch over their children. The multi-coloured horses, with eyes coming out of their sockets, appeared vaguely threatening. Only the young men playing volleyball on the sand court, with their muscular bodies and dexterity on full display, fit in snugly with the panorama of the beach scene.

'I'll go get a glass of water over there,' K. said, pointing to the ice cream shop. 'I'll also have to use the public toilets.'

R. nodded in silence, still engrossed in the otherworldly spectacle of the horses with mad eyes circling around in front of him. 'Go on, I'll wait for you here,' he answered in a daze.

As K. left him, R. noticed his brother's self-assured gait and wondered if it might be some kind of façade. It looked almost too perfect to be genuine. R. had one advantage over other people who knew K.—he had a common past with him as a member of the C. household. Underneath K.'s proud, sometimes even brazen airs, R. could still perceive the years of effort spent at building a persona designed precisely to appear proud and brazen. It was perfect but artificial, and relied on an intricate psychological mechanism which R. utilised as well, albeit less masterfully than his brother.

As his eyes were still scanning the surroundings while he was having those thoughts, R. happened upon an isolated man in a black suit sitting on a wooden bench, notepad in hand. With that black suit the man was sticking out like a sore thumb in the festive environment, so much so that his outfit seemed like a calculated move. Something about him indicated to R. that he wasn't from the region, though R. struggled to point the finger on why.

Urged on by a magnetic force of attraction, R. proceeded towards the stranger with careful steps. He stopped in his tracks a meter away from the bench.

Suddenly he felt that the man's aura repulsed him, and had repulsed him from the beginning. He thought that perhaps what had drawn him to that man was his inability to locate the source of his repulsion, like a slice of carrot cake that should logically appear delicious, except that it doesn't, despite our hunger.

The man turned towards R. and greeted him with a friendly smile, leaving his notepad on the side of the bench. It was a heartfelt yet reserved smile conveyed partly by the eyes which reminded R. of his own manner of smiling.

'A bit overdressed for a place like this, don't you think?' R. quipped.

At first the stranger just frowned at him in bewilderment. He couldn't have been older than twenty-five, though his outfit and facial features made him look older. He had a low forehead covered by a mass of brown curly hair, a snub nose, and a very arresting squint. R. reflected that he had never met anyone so spectacularly cross-eyed in his entire life.

'Poor devil,' he thought. 'He might be simple.'

But right at that moment the stranger's features shifted from puzzlement to benevolence.

'It's a strange habit I acquired in Oxford,' he replied. 'I became used to dressing formally in all circumstances. This doesn't bother me too much because I enjoy dressing this way. I am a busy man with very little free time, and the nature of my work demands that I wear a suit. Does this make sense to you?'

The tone of that question was not ironical but very candid. It seemed that the stranger was genuinely eager to get a bit of feedback from R. His accent was distinctly German, but he was extremely fluent in English and spoke very fast, though not at the sacrifice of precision. R. soon realised that he was the opposite of a simpleton.

'Why did you answer me in English? I asked my question in French,' R. said.

At this the stranger laughed uproariously. 'Why kind of question is that! You are very well-known around these parts, Mr. C.,' he replied, wiping his tears with a tissue.

R. was dumbstruck by the fact that the man knew his name. Surprise paralysed him and for a few seconds he could do nothing else than stare at the man who was staring back at him. His discreet, almost modest smile revealed a hint of curiosity sparked by R.'s agitation.

'Is something the matter?' the man enquired, blinking.

R. seized the opportunity of the distracting pair of eyes to bring himself back to focus.

'Why would I be well-known?' he asked in a barely audible whisper, looking at the ground, but the German's sharp ears picked up everything. He blinked his eyes even more to communicate his bewilderment, snatched his notepad, skimmed through it until he located the page he was looking for, then read some passage attentively for a few seconds. Whilst reading he looked up at R. several times at intervals, as if to check whether the portrait outlined on the page matched with R.'s face.

'Mmm,' his lips said without a sound. Suddenly the expression of deep pensiveness gave way to relief, and he smiled wide.

'I wasn't wrong!' he exclaimed joyously. 'You are due for an interview with us next week. I knew that I wasn't crazy. You had me wondering for a minute, Mr. C.'

The German noticed that R. was clenching his fists in reaction to his words. Fearing for his safety, he concealed his face behind his notepad. In that enterprise he was betrayed by the volume of his mane of hair, though his reaction was based on an overestimation of R.'s capacity for violence.

Discreetly he peered around the side of his notepad to check whether R. was about to attempt anything. He was reassured to see that R. had not moved an inch, but then he saw that R.'s lips were beginning to move.

'Why are you not dressed in dark blue?' R. asked at last, with the look of someone tortured by an impenetrable riddle.

'Dark blue? Why should I be dressed in dark blue?' the German answered, scratching and shaking his head. 'I don't even like that colour!'

But then, as if his actions were pre-coded in a software, his confusion shifted to serene amusement. Once again the corners of his mouth became convex.

'I see! You must be referring to my colleagues. Now that I think about it, some of them do have this quirk. But by no means all of them, oh no, by no means. I would say it's about fifty-fifty. On one side you have the eccentric folk with their blue suits, and on the other, well, I guess you have people like me,' he chuckled. 'How did the meetings go with these colleagues of mine, anyway?'

R. felt he had somehow anticipated those words, and without quite knowing why he regained his calm. He moved closer to the man and scrutinised him sternly.

'The joke isn't funny anymore. I warn you that there will be retributions if you go on.'

'What joke are you referring to?' the German replied candidly, gently stroking his notepad. 'I'm afraid I don't follow you, young man.'

It infuriated R. to be called 'young man' by that little gnome. 'To *that*!' he shouted, beside himself, while pointing successively to the notepad, the bench and the gentleman's own sibylline face. 'You have no right to be stalking me.'

R.'s annoyance was trying his nervous system, forcing him to breathe in deeply and noisily between his sentences. This did not fail to amuse his neighbour, which in turn annoyed R. even more. But R. didn't know what else to say, so he decided to say nothing for a while and just wait for the German's reaction.

From one of his jacket pockets the German drew out a cigarette and started making smoke rings.

'We don't mean to invade your privacy,' he said, looking up at the sky. But then instead of carrying on with his answer he just stopped and became completely engrossed in smoking. The movements of his fingers were so nonchalant that it almost seemed that R.'s exist-ence had become a matter of indifference to him.

'Like I said, this is not about privacy,' he resumed, 'but about testing your level of competence for the job. Having been through the application process, you are aware of how competitive this position is. Everybody wants it, or nearly everybody. In your own application you made it quite clear that you wanted it, too. You said that you were willing to put yourself at the 'entire dis-posal' of the organisation to show your dedication. I repeat: at the 'entire disposal' of, well, ourselves. Those were the words you used; I have them scribbled some-where in my notepad.'

Calmly he flicked through his notepad, cigarette in mouth, and easily located the evidence. Taking the ciga-rette out of his mouth, he read the sentence aloud with delight, much to R.'s mortification.

'I think this is rather clear,' the German said, nod-ding to himself. 'You really wanted the job, so you took the necessary measures. Hmm.'

He stopped again and felt his voice. 'You understand that our purpose isn't to drive you to the edge of a break-down. We just have very high standards. If you realise that you do not want to proceed, all you have to do is let us know and we will interrupt our inquiries right this mi-nute. But you should be aware that there is no way back.'

R. was now squatting in front of him, lost in thought. 'I'm still confused,' he said feebly. 'The inter-view is scheduled for next week. One of your secretaries rang me about it. Why are you testing me now if the in-terview is scheduled for next week?'

Blowing smoke rings with delicately curved lips, the German lent R. his ear casually, then gestured to him to ask if he was finished. 'Our secretary did not mislead you regarding the date and time of the interview,' he said. 'But you may have been guilty of not paying proper attention. The devil is in the details.'

'Not paying enough attention!' R. cried, infuriated by the accusation.

But the man raised his hand with authority to signal that he was not finished and wouldn't tolerate any further interruption. For the first time R. noticed that hint of annoyance in the German's behaviour, which both surprised and thrilled him.

'I was saying before you interrupted me,' the German resumed with nonchalance, 'that the standard by which a candidate stands out to an organisation like ours may differ from that of your average organisation. This is no insult to them, but simply reflects the nature and demands of our work. We consider that our candidates must demonstrate the ability to pick up what is left unsaid, as much as what is actually said. When you are at the epicentre of the Information Age the skill of reading between the lines is essential, but for us whose mission focuses specifically on the gathering of sensitive intelligence, that skill must be complemented by another, related yet distinct from it. This is the skill of reading *despite* the lines.' (The German laid great emphasis on that word.) 'Very few people can boast possessing that skill, which is why we are so eager to identify the candidates who do. Now, you may ask yourself what I mean by that skill, but my answer shall not surprise you in the slightest, especially if you still believe that you are a good fit for us.'

'Being the carrier of a secret truth is usually too big a burden for any human to handle. It is true that there are exceptions to be found among extraordinary men and women, but as a rule such individuals are incredibly rare, and we should consider ourselves lucky if we managed to recruit one every decade. By contrast, the world abounds with individuals tortured by the guilt of devious secrecy, whose sole dream, despite appearances occasionally kept up with great effort, is to divest themselves of their burden. Some of them will reveal only a partial truth, thinking a lie by omission less heinous than a straightforward lie. When dealing with these people the skill of reading between the lines comes into play, so that one can progress from the omission to the heart of the lie. But there are other people, almost as numerous but far less penitent, who are not content with simply lying by omission. They also can't resist peppering their half-truths with vulgar, blatant lies. What is to be done against those people? Well, you can now guess the answer. In such cases our staff must use the skill of reading despite the lines. When she spoke to you on the phone, our secretary, assuming that she really was a secretary, mentioned a date and a time for the interview. But do you not find it strange that she never mentioned a place? If you had read her despite the lines, you would have,' he concluded with a sigh, no longer smiling.

By that point R. was completely oblivious of his brother's lengthy absence. The squinting man's critique was claiming all of his attention.

'If I understand you correctly, the interview has already begun,' R. said sternly. 'But it still doesn't make sense that the secretary gave me a date and time for next week. She ought to have given me the date and time of the phone call itself since the interview effectively began at that point. Could it be that your secretary got confused?'

A distinct note of sarcasm coloured R.'s remarks, subtle but incisive, which did not fail to annoy the German. R. had noticed that his interlocutor knitted his brow every time he suffered a pique. As a result, the faintest movement of the German's eyebrows filled his heart with glee.

'It was neither a mistake nor an oversight,' the man said, quickly regaining control over himself, 'but a well-known stage in our recruitment process. Informally we like to call it the 'filling of the gaps', and the best candidates are invariably those who fill the deepest gaps. The fact that our secretary' (he laid peculiar emphasis on the word 'secretary') 'mentioned a date and time next week was only meant to distract your attention from her omission of an address. But even then, it wasn't such a devious trap. A time without a place! That should have stopped you in your tracks, but no, you merely nodded to yourself, said thank you to the secretary, and hung up. How strange... how very strange indeed.' The German was employing a tone of outright reproach.

'And what stage am I at now?' R. asked, uneasily trying to change the topic. His shoulders shrugged without asking permission from his will.

'Well, I'm not sure how to answer your question,' the German replied, lightly tapping his notepad with his right hand. 'I was only using a metaphor earlier when I referred to the different stages of the interview. It doesn't really break into discrete parts. Think about it as a continuum of different shades. At one extreme of the continuum, the interactions between the candidate and the organisation are very casual and informal and may take place anywhere, while at the other extreme is the final stage, the one that decides everything. Of course, this takes place at our headquarters, but only a tiny handful of candidates will be left by then.'

The man gave R. a knowing look, which seemed to say: 'I know this all sounds quite vague, but you understand that I can't say more or I would be unfairly helping you against the others.'

R. was lost in wonderment at this utterly alien manner of describing a process of recruitment. For a moment he believed himself to be stranded in a dream, but violently woke himself up by slapping his cheeks.

'You're still here,' he said to the German. 'So I must assume you weren't discouraged by my lack of discernment with your secretary. Otherwise you wouldn't have made the effort to come all the way to the south of ___ to spy on me. You're a busy man sacrificing some of your precious time for my sake, and strangely enough I am a little touched by that.'

To R.'s astonishment, the German reacted by overtly giggling to his face. And what curious giggles they were! They issued from his mouth in short, high-pitched bursts that sounded like a broken machine's final breaths.

'You are very audacious, Mr. C.,' he remarked between two spells of laughter.

Instinctively R. glanced behind his back to see if they were being noticed by the other visitors. In the interval the German recovered from his fit and was about to resume his train of thought, but when he saw that R. was no longer looking at him, he immediately got up from the bench and slipped behind R. unnoticed.

At that moment R. heard a shout coming from the other side of the carrousel.

'Come on, let's go!' K. shouted, waving at R. from a small distance, water bottle in hand. R. shouted back that he would be over in a minute, but when he turned around he saw with stupefaction the empty bench with the open notepad pushed to the side.

'So he's gone,' R. thought. He couldn't resist taking a peek inside the book, but the fact that it had been left there on purpose made him suspicious, so he kept his hands off it. Craning over the book he soon realised that he could not understand the bewildering language it contained. The pages, which were flying in the wind, were covered in esoteric symbols and childlike scribbles. R. shrugged his shoulders and went in pursuit of his brother, who was already striding towards the harbour.

'Where on earth had you disappeared to?' R. asked his brother as he caught up with him.

K. turned around and stared at R. with flashing eyes, his golden locks shining especially brightly in the sun. His expression, however, was sullen.

'That's my business,' he answered coolly. 'Who was that man anyway?'

'What about him?' R. said, feigning indifference.

K. was still looking at him with his piercing eyes. 'I saw you chatting to a man back there. Who was he? I don't think I've seen him before around these parts,' K. said, frowning.

R. shook his head. 'No, that was the first time I met him. As it happens, he also works for an organisation in ___. We just had a random encounter.'

'What is he doing here?' K. continued to inquire with insistence. R. was surprised by his brother's detective-like ways, which were very unusual for him. His heart disliked the feeling of being put on the spot.

'That would be too complicated to explain,' he replied, staring into the distance. 'You'd have to be familiar with the kind of microcosm that lives inside the walls of that city. He says that we met before at some event, and that we even talked briefly afterwards, but I remember neither him nor the event. This may well have happened. I have to attend so many of those, I tend to forget.'

R. was acutely conscious of his lying but he didn't find his lies abhorrent. The interview was none of K.'s business just in the same way that K.'s secret plans were none of R.'s business. The only thing R. lacked was the courage or the weariness to tell K. what K. himself had told him.

K. laughed sarcastically at his brother's words. 'A tooth for an eye, then,' he said with a knowing look, patting R. firmly on the shoulder.

The mistral wind had begun to blow much more powerfully. A tree was bent horizontally, nearly hitting K. in the face. The sea was starting to roar in a maelstrom of low, angry waves.

'The place is turning into an inverted graveyard,' R. said in a low voice. 'You can tell that a storm's coming.'

The force of instinct made him glance behind him once again. The carousel and its multi-coloured horses with mad eyes were still visible in the hazy distance. After some effort R. identified the bench where the German had been sitting, vacated and gloomy like a lost item about to be swept away by the storm. Scattered white objects with indistinct outlines were flying about the bench.

'Torn pages from the German's notepad,' R. thought, recalling the juvenile scrawls and the foreign symbols.

The rumbling sound of thunder interrupted his thoughts. Thick drops of rain were now lashing down.

'Let's get shelter over there,' K. said, grabbing R. by the arm and pointing at the awning of a shut restaurant whose name wasn't on display. The awning was already swollen with water but luckily the drops weren't yet passing through. In that little corner of safety R. went back to reminiscing about his meeting with the old man with the eagle eyes. Placid and immobile, he gazed without speaking at the flooding of the beach by the rainstorm. Already the streets were turning into sprawling mazes of puddles. The other pleasure-seekers, who had seemed so adventurous a few minutes earlier, had vanished from the premises. To go where? Only they knew.

'If only,' R. thought to himself so vividly that his lips were almost pronouncing the words in hushed sounds, 'if only that scene weren't so eerily familiar.'

Nonchalantly K. took out a pack of cigarettes from his pocket. With extremely precise movements that looked like the movements the characters in a painting by Boticelli would have made if they had been real people, he produced a lighter and began smoking. It was an expensive lighter, made of gold, that K. had inherited long ago from their father. Intrigued by the sight, R. lost himself in contemplation of the slowly decomposing cigarette held captive in K.'s lock of fingers.

'Doesn't it remind you of father?' R. asked, looking at the lighter. The taciturn figure on his right side, who was standing in the shade of the hidden corner, did not answer his question at first. Instead K. continued to alternate between taking drags from his cigarette and freeing it from the clasp of his lips, adroitly and even elegantly.

'You want to know the truth? I never thought about that at all,' K. said.

The shadows that were encircling K. gave his entire body the appearance of scowling. He held the lighter up to his eyes and scrutinised it closely.

'I guess I'll keep it,' he said, laughing. Underneath his laughter he was tightening his grip on the lighter.

'Of all the things I inherited from father, let me at least keep what I like,' K. continued, laughing more loudly still. The forced nature of that laugh made R. uneasy, but he found some solace in the fact the storm had driven people away, so nobody else would have to endure the strange noise.

R. would have liked to seize the occasion to ask K. if mending matters with their father was on the horizon, but at that moment the whole enterprise seemed as uncertain and slippery as the flooded pavements of the main street.

K. remained entirely absorbed in his cigarette, but that exaggerated sense of focus rang a false note. Since when had K. become so imperturbable? As he continued to scrutinise his brother in silence, R. noticed that under the faint light of the dying cigarette, K.'s fingers were shaking.

'Didn't you say earlier that you had plenty to tell me?' R. asked to break the silence.

K. threw away his cigarette butt and looked at him.

'I did say that,' he answered in almost a murmur. But he instantly raised his voice to protect his words from being drowned out by the wind. 'We should probably go home after the mistral has calmed down,' he said, deliberately changing the topic.

R. did not reply but looked at his brother with flashing eyes.

'Oh, yes! The big news. I'd nearly forgotten about that,' K. said with disarming lightness of heart. He opened his eyes wide to espouse a novel expression, which R. had never seen before, and said: 'I have decided not to talk to father ever again.'

'What do you mean, never again?' R. asked in a worried voice. 'Is this a figure of speech? There won't be any going back if you make a drastic move. You know the old man is very proud.' As he said those words, R. smiled inwardly. Deepest in his heart he considered pride a virtue rather than a sin, and felt grateful that he had inherited it.

'It's certainly not a figure of speech. My choice is made,' K. responded with clenched fist. 'After the man's heart surgery, I had a moment of clarity. You remember that I refused to call him and how the family judged me for it. I won't lie to you, the reaction of the others troubled me. I had thought they would understand my perspective. But all they could see were the words: heart, surgery. Almost from the beginning we knew it would be a routine operation. Father concealed this, of course, because he wanted everyone to feel sorry for him. But at the time I was unsure of myself. I asked myself questions. I wondered if I had been too harsh, and if behind that harshness I was only driven by resentment. However, that's not what dawned on me when I reached my moment of clarity.'

His eyes turned malignant, K. screwed up his mouth and said with evident glee: 'I realised that I couldn't give a damn what everyone else was thinking. It wasn't sadness that I was repressing, but guilt. I felt guilty that I didn't care. I realised then that I didn't care about what would happen to him. Trust me, if by accident he had died, I wouldn't have lost sleep over it.'

K.'s golden locks were flying in the wind with almost rebellious freedom. His dry, intense eyes gave his face a sharp look of self-assurance. It seemed that once spoken, the uneasy truth, far from reducing K. to tears, had been a huge relief to his nerves; and if he had cried it wouldn't have been from sadness, but from the physical explosiveness of that relief. The pressure released was immense and visible on K.'s body.

'I'm unhappy to hear that,' R. said, lowering his eyes. 'However, I'm not judging you for it. If you say that you won't change your mind, I have no right to try to convince you otherwise, even though I think it's a pity.' Those words were sincere, and K. knew it. He was aware of his brother's touching ingenuity in those moments. But K. also knew that R. was sad, very sad.

K. took out another cigarette, seemingly just to give his fidgeting hands something to play with. 'So this is all it is to you... a pity?' he asked in a strange voice, deep but somehow hollow, which did not fit the content of the question. R. was left out of sorts by that voice.

'No, no,' R. said, shaking his head more vigorously in his own perception than in reality. 'Pity is not the right word. It's something else and perhaps there's no word for it. I've no right to call it a pity, I'm not in your shoes.'

That last remark startled K. He took the cigarette out of his mouth and said in a barely audible whisper: 'Aren't you already in my shoes?'

That soft, hardly material utterance stroked R.'s cheek like a sabre. He stared at his brother gravely, then relaxed his facial muscles and began laughing.

'That's a good point,' he answered with feigned conviction. But as he noticed that K.'s expression was not echoing his own, he let the surface joy subside and became pensive again. 'But that's where the similarity ends,' he said, looking out at the stormy sea. 'I'm planning to confront him about what happened.'

K. felt a chill as he grasped that reference.

Soon after the mistral began to quiet down; it was still blowing into the brothers' faces but more softly, with a touch of nurturing care not unlike that of the sea.

'I understand,' K. said, following R.'s gaze into the crooked horizon. 'If this is what you think you must do, then you should do it. Follow your instinct.'

R. clenched both of his fists. 'It is time. I feel ready. Everything in me has changed for the better since the news of the interview. I am afraid, but also full of strength.'

In that moment of quiet, contained enthusiasm, R. looked over the fact that he hadn't told K. about the interview. With raised eyebrows K. looked at him and let his gaze hover about for a while.

'Well, I guess he's no longer happy with his job. A good thing he's got an opportunity elsewhere,' K. thought. Obviously K. couldn't have known how short his estimate was falling, but R. noticed his brother's unmoved reaction and was secretly annoyed by it.

Then, still without thinking, K. came back with another deadly stab. 'I'm sure you already know that father isn't around at the moment,' he said candidly, unaware that his words were utterly dismantling his brother's covert plans. 'Mother mentioned that he was on a business trip to Corsica. He won't be back before the end of the month.'

R. looked at his brother with chattering teeth and an expression of disgust. He was beginning to shake all over.

'You think this is funny?' he asked, seething with anger. 'Is that how you entertain yourself? Don't you have better things to do than making up stories to wind me up?'

Instinctively K. took a step backwards. He was familiar enough with that instinct to know that fear was the cause of it. An acute observer of human behaviour, K. was aware that the bravest of men rarely had to be feared; on the contrary it was the emasculated, those that boiled with a suppressed anger that would not let itself out, who were capable of the worst deeds. Suddenly a memory flashed through K.'s mind. He pictured the philosopher Louis Althusser, celebrated in his own lifetime as a giant of the discipline, coldly strangling his wife in a moment of madness. That was what K. feared, and his fear was heightened by his keen understanding of his brother.

'He'll be back in a month,' K. said hesitantly.

But it was too late. R. was clenching his fists so hard with nervous agitation that the bones in his fingers and wrists made a series of horrible cracking noises. His deep blue eyes, which had remained concealed by the ambient darkness until then, were now protruding from their sockets, swelling with venomous intensity. His mouth was almost paralysed, but at the price of colossal effort he whispered: 'Life is a joke... so why am not allowed to laugh like everyone else?'

K., who was glued against the wall at the maximal distance from R., did not know what to answer; or rather he knew that there was nothing to say. He had witnessed those fits in the past, but the past had taught him precisely the opposite of a moral lesson. It had taught him that nothing could be done except run away. Although the real cause of the fits lay elsewhere than in words, the danger that arose from them was close at hand.

'Tell me,' R. said ominously, 'why you don't experience those fits anymore. What is your secret? I want to know.'

Incapable of hiding an expression of dismay, K. said that he had no explanation. But R. insisted with such covert vehemence that K. had to say something, anything, to try to calm his brother. But he was luckless in not having the skill to wrap his sentences in a fabric softer than the words themselves.

Shrugging in a way that was not commanded by his brain but by a sudden eruption of spasms in his upper back, K. said what he sincerely believed to be the truth.

'I stopped suffering from those fits when I decided to part ways with father completely. Not when I made myself believe that I had parted ways with him, but when I actually felt the conviction running through my veins. I can't tell you how I managed to hold on to that conviction. It just happened, one morning after a cigarette on the balcony, and from then onwards everything was changed.'

As he spoke those words K. had not the courage to look at his brother in the face. The price to pay for his honesty was cowardice, he thought, and in having that thought he found relief in the satisfaction that his words were genuine. What his cowardice shielded him from was R.'s bloodshot eyes staring at him with jaw hanging loose and the corners of his mouth foaming with saliva.

'I haven't given up,' R. spat out, producing a frightening gurgling noise with his throat. 'You have, but I haven't. It's just that fate seems to be against me. It won't let me confront father. And it won't even let me laugh!' he bellowed, striking his chest. 'Can you imagine the torture of not being able to laugh a good, guttural laugh? Ha ha ha ha ha ha!'

Now R. was laughing hysterically in a forced and exaggerated manner. His brother was extremely alarmed by that new phase in R.'s hysteria. Forgetting all about fraternal care in the fraction of a second, K. ran away into the surrounding fog with the speed of a deserter.

In the meantime R. had dropped flat on the floor and was shaking all over with convulsions. The veins on his neck and forehead were protruding in a vile, ugly spectacle of pain. But as he suffered through his fit R. could not help thinking of how unfair it was that even his own brother had abandoned him like a discarded toy. With bitterness he reflected that he was alone, misunderstood and helpless. Somehow it wasn't K.'s desertion so much as the fact that K. no longer had those fits that hurt him the most. And then there was that thought about laughter—an intrusive, nagging thought that wouldn't leave his mind. 'Why can't I laugh? How can I respect myself if I can't even mock myself?'

*****

The rest of the weekend was uneventful. By the time he returned home R. was soaked to the bone but psychically relieved, his nerves having exhausted themselves of the capacity to burn. Without even paying attention to who was in the house he climbed upstairs and left himself fall into a hot, steaming bath.

Only later did it turn out that K. had not waited for him before driving back to ___. 'It's a shame K. won't be dining with us tonight, we see so little of him these days,' R.'s mother said in a bittersweet understatement. She was talking about herself, of course. R. guessed that the attitude of downcast submission to fate his mother wore at all times was due at least in part to the infrequency of K.'s visits. Her suffering in itself wasn't strange, but the extent of it was.

'I can't hear you properly through the door, I'm taking a bath,' R. answered curtly, but his words were muffled by the steam.

The abruptness of that answer signalled a lack of compassion on R.'s part, and had three causes. The first was entirely physical. R. had been looking forward to that bath ever since he lifted himself up from under the awning of the unnamed shop, and considered it his just reward. The bath was to him what a paradisal island would be to the survivor of a shipwreck. Above all else he was looking forward to peace and serenity. But now his mother has cast a spanner in the works by uttering her saddened remark about K.'s absence.

The second reason was linked to the first. R.'s lack of patience with his mother's quiet lament did not motivate him to enter into conversation. His brother was gone: so be it! That was K.'s style, after all. Perhaps R. would pay him a visit later in town. And then there wouldn't be revenge but simply forgetting, because the members of the C. family liked to think that nothing strange ever happened between them. Perhaps it was too difficult to see things otherwise, because if they saw things otherwise they would immediately have to accept the fact of their strangeness. R. did not deny to himself the fact that K. had escaped from him, but he also knew that in the distant past, maybe he had one or twice escaped from K.

The third reason was both the most obvious and the most difficult to confess, though R.'s mother saw it and chose to ignore it, having no alternative. It was Jealousy with a capital J, owing not to its intensity but to the strenuous effort with which it was repressed, as were so many other aspects of R.'s life. With heart-wrenching lucidity he observed that his mother hardly lamented his own absence. It was so intriguing to him, and as the same time so perplexing, that he himself should be closer to his mother, but that his mother should still love K. more. It was a fact devoid of any hard evidence save the visceral feelings of a son given second place, like the finalist of a tennis tournament, praised, applauded and even loved, but still coming second place.

Although R. often thought to himself that K. didn't deserve being the preferred one, he knew deep down that matters of the heart have little to do with questions of rational reward. His mother's preference was arbitrary in its essence, irrational but unquestionable. It was not open to doubt because it could be seen and had no need of discussion. R. found some solace in knowing that he was his grandmother's favorite; but that sense of solace didn't last long, because a grandmother isn't a mother. When all is said and done, it is only the mother's feelings that count.

'I'm taking a bath, mother, I can't hear you!' R. shouted at the top of his lungs, or rather what was left of his lungs. He had no intention of telling her about his fit. 'Why would I?' R. thought. He already knew that his mother's only possible response was an expression of concern of genuine but low intensity. And he would compare the feebleness of her response, endowed with a limited lifespan, to her seemingly endless grief at the thought of K.'s infrequent visits.

So instead of drowning in those negative thoughts, R. drenched himself in the steaming water. He relished the sensory pleasure it gave to his bruised and wrinkled skin, which seemed to him a cathartic relief from the pains of the day. 'In the solitude of a hot bath,' he whispered to himself with a smile, 'almost anyone can live.'

*****

Instead of a night out, R. chose to spend the evening writing. For a few months now he had been working on a novel based on his experience living in ___. When people asked him about that project he felt excited but remained vague, as he didn't want to give away too much too quickly. In his mind his work had to remain shrouded in secrecy.

One of the reasons was that his account of the city and its people was critical to the point of being callous; but there were other, more subterranean reasons of which he was not entirely conscious. For one, the idea that he had the power to let people know about the content of his manuscript but deliberately refrained from it imbued his mind with a sense of permanent danger which boosted his energy for writing.

Somehow that logic didn't apply to his close friends, to whom he would have told everything they wanted to know, no matter the risk of spoiling their enjoyment of the book. The idea of sharing his written misdeeds with trustworthy relations appealed to him as much as it frightened him to do the same with mere acquaintances. He knew that his project was an exercise in transgression, and found pleasure in the image of old norms being bent and broken by his own hands. But for that very reason he was also concerned about possible repercussions on his social life both present and future.

Sometimes R. asked himself what he would say to those trusted friends who expressed interest in the book within the confines of his imagination. In those moments he realised with heightened awareness and a hint of pain in his heart that he was at a loss for an answer. This was a real problem because sooner or later, his ambitions would compel him to actually promote the book. The main hurdle was that the story's main character was an alternate version of himself—a counterpart from another world, nearly identical to R. in appearance but of a darker and more unforgiving temperament. It was hard for R. to imagine showing this character to the public. On occasion he even felt uneasy at the idea of having created that being.

He had originally called his story a dystopia, which was a concept in vogue at the time and a nod to some of his favourite works of art. But through repeated exposure to his own act of writing he became more familiar with the motivations that underlay his narrative, and he came to realise that the word *dystopia* did not describe his story very well. The word didn't do justice to what was perhaps the most unique aspect of the work. On the surface, the bulk of his narrative was about the mundane events of an average man's everyday life; very little about it seemed worthy of a work of fiction. But slowly and impercepti-bly the descriptions blended with the protagonist's subjective interpretations of their content. It was done so seamlessly that the reader would struggle to distinguish fact from fiction. To confuse the reader in that way while simultaneously compelling him to continue reading was R.'s purpose. He wanted the reader's state of confusion to foster curiosity and the desire to know the end of the story. Simultaneously R. wanted the overall effort to be not easy, but strenuous and uncertain.

There was also the fact that R.'s intimacy with his protagonist established between them an almost entirely instinctual relationship not based on mutual understand-ing but rather on affect. That relationship was so unanalytical that it filled R. with joy. At no point did he have to ask himself: 'What would I do if I found myself in that situation?' because he had found himself in that situation. The future of his protagonist was his own past, while their respective lives met only in the present.

R. enjoyed unmediated access to the wide spectrum of emotion possessed by his protagonist. He was able to pull this lever, push that button, effortlessly and indeed unthinkingly, for no thought was involved. Such psychological realism was a great asset to him as a writer, but it also made it quite challenging to speak about the book to other people in simple, rational language. Whenever a questioner put him on the spot, R. always anticipated that his response would disappoint, because he didn't have a response. Instead he would have liked to raise his hand and point his finger to his temple. With that gesture he would say: 'If only you could read my mind, you would understand.'

After two hours of strenuous writing, R. took a break and headed downstairs to get himself some tea. He took his time to pour water from the tap into a small pot and heated it to make it boil. Instead of waiting lazily in front of the stoves he went and fetched the only teabag he found in the cupboard, placing it delicately at the bottom of his favourite cup. The face of Thomas Jefferson was painted on its side, with the quote: 'Power is not alluring to pure minds.' R. thought those words conveyed a universal truth about human beings. In his eyes the man of pure mind did not have to be especially lovable nor even admirable. He had only to be pure; and purity was the wellspring of virtue, the enemy of power.

R. greatly admired Thomas Jefferson as a historical figure. As president of the United States he thought Jefferson had embodied an impressive reconciliation between power and purity of mind. When looking at the long career of that illustrious man it was tempting to deem him passive and overly idealistic, but each time what appeared like passivity and idealism were only the outward expression of a reluctance to exert power super-fluously, combined with an ability to see far and clearly into the future. Jefferson had been one of those men who knew when to wait, and who always struck at the right moment, like a fencer. With a smile coloured by antinational feeling R. recalled how Napoleonic France, whilst cornered on all sides by its enemies, had had to sell Louisiana to the United States for a pittance. Jefferson had waited, and then Jefferson had struck. It was only at the critical moments that his unique talent had expressed itself, summoned by the call of history. It had been a talent more akin to a sharp laser than a nuclear blast.

As he poured the hot water into the cup, R. thought he saw his reflection on the surface; and the shock of it brought him back to the reality of his condition. He wasn't Jefferson. But perhaps he could be something different, respectable in its own way. R.'s adeptness at finding counterarguments to his own ideas led him to wonder if the reason for his feeling of inferiority might not be that his soul was, after all, more innocent than Jefferson's—and therefore purer.

R. brought the cup to his lips. The savour of green tea delighted his taste buds. 'If only I could write a book like that,' he thought. 'A book of warm, subtle taste, which would be food for the soul. I dream of writing something tasteful and warm, authored by a pen dipped in lava ink.'

Immediately his mind wandered into memories of reading Dostoyevsky's novels, especially *Crime and Punishment*. It was a book that overflowed with love and forgiveness, and R. hoped to accomplish something in that vein. He knew that his style was immature, that it needed spirit; but more important was the aim to develop his own voice.

As he sipped on his tea, R. began to wonder if an author's voice could really be separated from his spirit. He could find no rational answer to that question; but the cast of his mind was such that instead of giving up, he began looking for an irrational answer instead. Gradually and inevitably, he found himself replaying in his mind the news about the interview.

Things were getting to a head now, a fact which he almost found hard to believe. Rarely had he experienced such a sense of anticipation. The next day he would be heading back to ___; this time, however, he was planning to spend the entire train journey studying for the interview. He had to make sure that he was ready for the big event. And that meant practice, practice, practice.

His unease of a few days ago had ripened into something opposite to his original feeling. He now felt confident and full of strength. The set of odd characters he had encountered since the news of the interview had become a mere variable in his mind's eye, and one he had become accustomed to. 'Let them throw themselves at me and try to stop me if they dare,' he thought. For a second he could not believe that such a thought had occurred to him, but he made peace with that idea quite effortlessly. The lonely fit under the rain-soaked awning had caused in him a change whose source was unknown, but whose effect was so tangible that it threatened to burst his heart open.

*****

The fateful week had come. On his way to work R. was surprised to find the tram half empty, and still more surprised at himself for not noticing it sooner. For the first few minutes upon entering the tram he had been musing about the interview in a very positive mindset, bathing in the exceptionally sunny weather. The ill-shaped clouds of the day before had dissolved, leaving behind them a gorgeous expanse of bright blue dotted here and there with the white, elongated figures of planes.

R. felt a rush of adrenaline pumping through his veins as he breathed in every particle of that unique, rarefied air. Eagerly he looked round him for his fellow passengers to share in his rapture, forgetting in his drunkenness that he was alone. Only then did he recall that he was going to work earlier than usual, at a time when the streets of __ were still deserted. R. thought of the old lady in the train and the joy that she would feel at the sight of the sky. He pictured her crying tears of happiness mingling with the colour of the sky and blotting her black dress with invisible stains.

As R. entered the office he saw Mr. Axel standing at the back of the hall, alone and pensive by the coffee machine. The noise produced by the opening of the door, though kept quiet by R.'s skinny arm, tickled Axel's sensitive ears. He turned around and glanced at R. with his youthful candour, which was already invading every inch of his face. He got ready to hold his hand out.

'Look who's here! How was your weekend, Mr. C.?' Axel asked from across the room, the palm of his hand already opened wide. He had the playful habit of addressing his colleagues by their family names.

'Very good, and how was yours?' R. said, walking towards him with measured steps. He saw Axel open his mouth, but exactly at that moment the coffee machine began to grind and hiss as it poured the coffee into a cardboard cup. The resulting noise muted Axel's juvenile voice. R. nodded to him with a knowing look to give him the impression that he had listened.

Once in the vicinity of the coffee machine, R. realised that he had been craving caffeine all morning. He typically failed to heed the signals given by his body until those signals became pressing. In another corner of his field of vision he saw the hand of Mr. Axel extended to him, and shook it with a firmness intended to cover up his lack of interest. What R. didn't see was that the unusual sensation was not lost on the perspicacious Axel.

Without really trying to sustain the conversation, R. pressed the button to pour himself a cup of coffee. The experience of seeing the machine produce a brand new cup every time the button was pressed gave him great pleasure, though he couldn't say why. To him it seemed a miracle that the machine, which was not much bigger than a black cube, could contain such an impressive number of cups. The only thing he didn't like was the squishing noise involved in the process, which grated his ears and made him grind his teeth nervously.

This time the noise produced was even shriller than usual and made him start. Awareness of the little jump he made led his eyes back to Axel. Instinctively he wanted to say: 'That machine sure has a temper!' but he didn't say that, because Axel's expression of deep sullenness, which was new to him, perplexed and confused him. His manager was scowling at him and anxiously twisting his mouth.

'Are the rumours true?' he queried R. in a tone of reproach. An entirely new, hitherto unknown version of Axel was unveiling itself to him.

'What rumours?' R. answered curtly. He kept a steely outside but internally the strain on his nerves was already painful.

Axel stared at him with watery eyes. 'The rumours about your plans to leave us for another place,' he said ruefully. 'After all we've done for you!'

Having said those words he burst out crying, failing on his knees and snivelling like a child trying to elicit a reaction from his parents.

R. walked to his manager and patted his shoulder in silence. Mr. Axel's sobbing was loud and somewhat embarrassing, but it also exhibited an eerily regular pattern, alternating between lower and higher pitches, and even what sounded like musical motifs in staccato. Not knowing whether his aching to see his manager in that state stemmed from pity or disgust, R. chose instead to bathe in the sensory pleasure given him by the melody of the sobs.

'Even if I were to look for opportunities elsewhere, what would be wrong about that?' R. said, spurred by the growing silence and the desire to collect his cup of coffee.

Axel took a deep breath and straightened himself up. His face was still overcome with vexation but his eyes had dried up, though for the moment he refused to look at R.

'Nothing's wrong on paper,' he said, 'but all the same, the mere thought of it is shocking. You seem to forget that we are… a family,' he whispered wistfully, turning round to gaze into R.'s eyes with an air of deep devotion.

'What nonsense!' R. cried, goaded to anger by the preposterous premise. His eyes flashed with an intimidating glare. 'Do you listen to yourself when you speak? I work here because I get paid, and so does everyone else. How dare you imagine that I would feel bound to this organisation?'

The attempt by Axel to creep into his personal life exasperated R. beyond belief. With regained self-control he turned his back on Axel without waiting for a response and walked to the coffee machine.

'Wait, you churlish brute!' Axel shouted in protest at R.'s ignoring him. As he said those words he threw his hand at R. from behind and grabbed his left shoulder to pull him back. Axel could not have anticipated the consequences of his desperate attempt. When R. felt that foreign hand landing on his shoulder he was immediately reminded of his altercation with the old man with the eagle eyes. The force of defensive instinct made him swivel back and pack a vicious punch in his manager's chin. Axel instantly collapsed on the floor, knocked unconscious.

'Jesus, what have I done!' R. gasped, overcome by panic. With the timidity of a wrongdoer he scanned the room to confirm the absence of witnesses. Wasting no time he bent his knees, grabbed the inert body of Axel by the shoulders and tugged him across the floor to his office. He was brought to a pitch of lucidity he had never expected possessing. At the price of colossal physical effort he managed to lift his manager into his chair and turned on his computer, so that to a newcomer's untrained eye things might look as if Mr. Axel was merely taking a morning nap.

With the swiftness of a gymnast R. raced back to his own office and sat down in front of his computer. He felt his chest with his hands, crossed himself—he could not remember the last time he had crossed himself—and breathed in deeply. At that moment it occurred to him that in the last five minutes he had not been thinking at all; his body had applied itself with deftness to obeying the immediate demands of the situation. R. was impressed by that realisation because he had no idea that he was capable of such a feat. He also couldn't have anticipated how pleasurable it felt.

'I'll act as if nothing happened. With a bit of luck Axel won't remember anything,' R. said to himself as he scrolled down the list of messages saturating his email box. He glanced at the clock above him, which indicated a quarter past eight. He knew that within a few minutes the office would begin to fill up with a small number of punctilious coworkers.

The morning sun's rays were shining with almost menacing intensity. Irritated by the sensory aggression,

R. got up from his chair and paced to the wall behind him to lower the blinds. The feeling of guilt made the interval of time during which he pulled the blinds down seem infinitely long, but at last he tasted darkness in the air he was breathing, and immediately felt better.

On the way back to his chair and with his sense of sight regained, R. perceived a change in the environment. The path from the physical stimulus to the coherence of thought was obstructed by the singular nature of that change. For a second R.'s own consciousness lost sight, groping its way about in the grey-back halo between sleep and wakefulness. He blinked his eyes several times to make out the scene's unfamiliar setup.

There was Milena, standing straight by the office door. She was looking at him with a blank expression kept alive only by the tiniest fragment of curiosity, in the same way that people look at strangers with indifference during a walk through a park.

But then R. realised that Milena was not actually staring at him. She was looking in his direction, but not quite at him, and the realisation made him feel like an obstacle. It was an extremely unpleasant sensation. Incapable of holding out any longer, R. sank silently into his chair. With some effort he succeeded in lifting his head up to face her. Her obsidian eyes were eating his flesh.

'What are you standing over there for, Milena? Come in or you'll block the passage for the person I'm waiting for', he said with an impatient gesture beckoning her to clear the way. By appearing to be impatient he also hoped to disguise his obvious lie. He was waiting for nobody.

Suddenly R. began to hear the muffled sound of steps pacing up the stairs outside the office. The heavy handle of the entrance door made its familiar cracking noise upon being turned, and now R. heard that noise without knowing what to make of it. A few more minutes passed, marked by the utter stillness of the two bodies that populated R.'s office. Only the sound of steps continued and became louder and more frantic, punctuated by long, frustrated sighs.

'Milena!' a powerful female voice shouted from the hall. 'The coffee machine appears to be broken. Would you mind calling customer service? Good morning, by the way.' R. recognised the authoritative timbre of the director of communications.

Milena's eyes immediately recovered their habitual expression of servility. 'Of course, I'll take care of it presently!' she said in a sheepish tone, running back into the hall with the haste of a servant. R. wanted to breathe deeply and stretch his arms, but instead he shrugged his shoulders and had a scornful thought or two about his colleague.

The day flew by at great speed. As he was about to leave the office R. got a phone call. The secretary from the other organisation, not even caring to say hello, informed him that the interview was to take place that evening. With a trembling hand R. wrote down the address of the organisation. 'I advise you to leave now,' the secretary said, and hung up.

*****

R. hadn't expected the headquarters of the organisation to be located at the heart of the city centre. Its large oval building was planted on the other side of the train station, closer to the lake. R. had gazed at it from his office window more than once, mistaking it for the seat of a United Nations agency. The building looked very new and couldn't have been older than ten or fifteen years old. Like the Petal Building it was almost entirely made of glass, but it was higher by ten or fifteen floors, and the glass walls were of a vaguely translucid dark green colour. Maybe the employees inside were able to keep an eye on the outside world, but they themselves couldn't be seen.

For once the autumn season was on R.'s side. As soon as he slipped out of the Petal Building the sky covered his body with a thick layer of darkness. The almost tangible weight of that new clothing reminded him of the time when he had gone home full of pride after the news of the interview. That time seemed to belong to a distant past, and yet it had only been four days. When R. made the calculation he was astonished at the process of contraction that had taken place inside his mind. Those four days had felt to his like a lifetime in miniature.

To get to the oval building R. had to cross the entire length of the train station from north to south and glide down steep steps to a large parking lot deserted by cars, at the other end of which he could see one of the side entrances to the building. He came down the steps carefully and busily made his way across the parking lot.

It would have been difficult to picture an emptier landscape than the compact collection of those desolate props. As for the oval building, the atmosphere of quiet tension that surrounded it was merely a symptom caused by R.'s own knowledge of the interview. He could feel that tension pumping through his veins, and he liked it.

The side entrance door had a sign posted next to it, whose makeshift appearance did not look very professional. On it was written: 'FOR THE INTERVIEWS – THIS WAY.' Upon getting closer, R. couldn't grasp why the route to such an important event should be through the puniest door in the whole building. It was barely the size of a regular house door, made of the building's trademark thick green glass. R. grabbed the handle and tried to turn it, but he realised that the door was locked.

'Impossible,' he thought. 'How can it be locked if I have to go through it? This doesn't make sense.'

He began hyperventilating as the thought occurred to him that the interview sessions had most likely started already. If so, then perhaps the confusing sign ought to be read not at face value, but 'despite the lines,' as per the German's expression, which R. repeated under his breath. Perhaps the whole point was to interpret the sign by reversing its meaning. At a loss for other options, R. decided to take a walk around the building in search of the proper entrance.

On the strength of his intuition R. avoided the main door. After a moment of hesitation he reckoned that the choice would be too obvious and was sure to lead to another impasse. Under the dazzling light he saw the slim figures of people coming out, but none of them was coming in.

'Wrong direction, wrong door,' he whispered to himself with a clenching of his fists. 'My goal is not just to enter the building. It is to be selected, and to be selected I must avoid that door.'

R. took a right into the engulfing darkness of a grassy plot that circled the other side of the oval building. Even in broad daylight that side was concealed from view by the skyscrapers and the train station. Undaunted, R. began to skirt the building in the total darkness, feeling his ankles being tickled by low-lying bushes. He was groping his way about by flailing his arms wildly and randomly in front of him. Only the sound of his feet stomping the grass and the flinging of his arms into the void could be heard. The noise of cars driving and honking in the distance, just like the serene humming of the train station, had vanished from his auditory field.

The absence of visible landmarks deprived R. of the ability to measure exactly how far he was advancing in time and space. 'Is this how the world feels to God?' he asked himself with a smile.

He walked nearly blindfolded for another fifty meters until at last a small moving object of yellowish colour popped into his field of vision. It did not look like much, hesitant and indistinct as it was in the fog of ghastly yellow; and yet R. felt at that moment that a fabulous treasure was offering itself up to him.

Upon closer inspection, the object turned out to be a lantern perched upon a rusty metallic door, which was very much unlike the polished emerald of the rest of the building. Inching closer to the lantern, R. made out that the door was built into a concrete patch of wall extended for around fifteen meters on both sides.

R. seized the door handle with his cold, dry hand. This time the handle let itself be turned like a charm. 'Open, sesame!' R. exclaimed joyously.

With a creaking noise the door slowly opened under the pressure of R.'s arm. It gave access to a lightless corridor at the end of which another door could be vaguely guessed at, a little distance away. The faint rays of light beaming shyly round the sides seemed an indication that the room behind that other door was bright and teeming with people. Without a trace of hesitation R. penetrated into the corridor, pushing the door shut behind him. The sheer physical effort he had to make to close that door left him panting for a while. He asked himself whether he would even find the strength to pull it open again, but quickly forgot about that worry.

R. almost stunned himself with the thought that the tunnel in front of him ought to have crushed him with claustrophobic terror, had it not been for that faint glimmer of light breathing through the sides of the second door, distant and detached yet also serene. Its presence, no matter how intangible, sufficed to vanquish the blackness completely. R. reflected further that the good life so cherished by moral philosophers, assuming that it was attainable, was probably not very different from that dark tunnel rendered bearable by the hope of light.

The presence of the timid rays also meant that within the confines of the corridor, R. was no longer thrown out of space and time. He had a path to follow, a physical destination to reach. That point in material space, which he wasn't able to touch yet, meant simultaneously a point in time. And behind the revived coordinates of space and time was concealed the warmest of human feelings, which R. now experienced. It was the feeling of belonging to the world, of simply being at home in it.

Like a man secretly convinced that death was imminent, R. took his time to relish every single one of the steps he had to make to get to the second door. But in an instant he was already in front of it, stroking its smooth handle like a lover would the wrist of his mistress, smiling to himself and trying to picture what his smile would convey to the people he was about to greet. Then, without warning, he grabbed the handle firmly, turned it twice, and opened the door.

*****

The stark transition from near complete blackness to a space extravagantly furnished with lights left R. blind for a minute. When at last he cautiously drew his arm away from his eyes, he saw that nobody was there to greet him and felt disappointed. But that nascent feeling quickly subsided and gave way to a mixture of perplexity and fascination. The little door, which he was now able to examine under the lights, was made of the same glassy green as the walls of the oval building. R. saw in it an unmistakable sign that he was back in interview territory.

What he still did not understand was why the place looked so deserted. The green door opened onto a massive hall bordered by polished wooden walls. The floor was covered in blue carpet and looked very new. R. squatted down to smell the carpet from close up, his eyes beaming with curiosity. 'It's definitely quite new,' he observed with a nod.

He made a number of other remarks to himself from his scanning of the interior of the building, in a loud voice made secure by the absence of witnesses. To his surprise his voice echoed noisily against the partitions of the building, and upon hearing himself he felt shame.

Suddenly another voice came out of a speaker planted above the green door.

'Welcome to our headquarters, Mr. C. We were beginning to wonder if you had changed your mind.' The timbre of that voice was familiar to R. It belonged to the German with the squinty eyes. R. looked around him by a kind of reflexive gesture, but found nothing changed in the environment.

'We are very happy to see you among us this evening,' the voice continued. 'Why don't you come and join us upstairs? If you look to your left towards the northern end of the corridor, you will see a flight of stairs about fifty meters from where you are. The stairs are entirely made of glass, so you may not notice them at first. Try to be swift but careful with your movements. Once you make it to the stairs, walk up to the third level, take a right and proceed through the narrow corridor to the large office space on the right hand side. At that point you should be able to see us through the glass partition. We shall be welcoming you at the door. The final stage of the interview will follow shortly after.'

R.'s body shivered all over at the mention of the interview. The final stage, he said! R. felt that the most important episode of his life was about to unfold. In his excitement he forgot for a moment that on the interview panel were to be two individuals he had skirmished with. As he paced across the hall, that mysterious truth suddenly struck him, brought to light by the German's velvety voice. But R. no longer feared anyone. He felt as if the man who had come out of the black corridor was a reformed version of himself.

The way up presented R. with few obstacles. The only dilemma he encountered was that of deciding whether to stop at the third or fourth floor. He had to stop at the third, of course, and he remembered that very well; but all the levels looked exactly the same and in his haste R. made the silly, inexperienced error of neglecting to keep a count of each one of them. He couldn't ask anyone for help either, since nobody was to be found anywhere. R. rushed down to the bottom of the stairs and hurried back up with the intent to ascribe an ordinal number to each new level he reached.

When finally he reached the third level he took a sharp right turn; in front of him the slim corridor snaked its way to the northern tip of the building. After a brief pause, R. resumed his stride forward with determination. He knew what was awaiting him, around the corner, inside the big office.

The path down the hallway meandered without variation, threatening him with the loss of his bearings once again. 'The office on the right hand side, with the transparent wall of glass,' he kept repeating to himself as a

129

mnemonic device. That rudimentary tactic helped him to impose a form on the endless succession of empty offices with glass partitions on the left hand side, while on the right hand side there was the wooden wall with its usual polished sheen.

That section of the wall was dotted with scattered posters in black and white which showed the faces of people R. didn't know, with an accompanying caption written in an unknown language. R. was especially struck by the regular appearance of symbols and scribbles around those short lines of unintelligible text.

'The German's notepad,' he observed to himself. The similarity was unmistakable. 'He must have quite a senior role in the organisation. Unless this is a secret language that everyone here speaks to communicate confidential information.'

The faces displayed on those poorly printed posters shared a uniformly sullen expression, but that sullenness seemed only to be a mask for a disposition more buried, and for that reason more unnerving. None of them looked happy, but they did not exactly look sad either. Rather their expressions seemed to convey a perfect absence of emotion—an incapacity for human feeling blended with a curious sense of pride about being thus incapacitated which transpired subtly in their eyes. R. was entertained by the paradox of a person showing pride at lacking feeling, since pride itself, prior to being a sin, is a state of feeling pervading body and soul, which the human mind only rationalises later in the language of causes and symptoms.

Soon after the posters vanished entirely from the wall, as if an invisible line of demarcation had been agreed upon internally by the staff, beyond which the wood was to be kept in as pristine a condition as possible. As a new visitor to the organisation, R. was only able to faintly intuit the vast, intricate web of rules and practices that the staff had come to abide by, some of them imposed from above, others more horizontal and building up over long periods of time through a process of accretion. On the other side the long, tedious series of empty offices offered him a dreary view of monotonous sameness. The desks were disposed exactly in the same way inside each office, each equipped with carbon copies of a white laptop pasted on to an endless sequence of identical images. There wasn't a single trace of a personal item anywhere—a hat, a scarf, a family portrait or a Christmas calendar, the possibilities were as infinite as they were unrealised in that chilly wasteland.

Then at last the offices, bored to excess by their own presence, gave way to a long section of wooden wall. 'Some change, finally!' R. thought. He was so relieved by that tiny speck of change that he even doubted for a second that it was real. He pulled up on the left hand side to carefully inspect the new section of wall, rubbing it delicately with the palm of his hand and pressing his face close to the surface to smell the scent of wood. 'Definitely real wood,' he confirmed with a smile.

At that moment he made a jump at the sound of a door opening in his vicinity. It wasn't a loud noise, but the clash of its creeping proximity with the rest of the absentee building made it aggressive to R.'s ears. He turned around without flinching and set about looking for the source of the noise.

He didn't have to look very far. On the opposite side of the corridor, facing him with smiles of various shapes, the three individuals of the week before were standing outside the office with the glass partition. Inside that office was an imposing glass table designed to reproduce the shape of the oval building. The members of the interview panel approached him with carefully measured steps.

'It is a great pleasure to meet you in person again,' said the German, extending a welcoming hand. But at first R. didn't notice that hand. His field of vision was overwhelmed by the presence of the man with the eagle eyes.

He felt drawn to the old man by a kind of magnetic attraction. Leaning casually against the wall with his head slightly lowered, the man was staring at R. with a suspicious expression which, however, didn't seem as hostile as it used to be. His wide, wrinkled forehead, almost too heavy for him to carry around, looked nobler than ever under the bright lights of the corridor. For a second R. wondered if the two of them had known each other in a distant past.

Suddenly R. felt his hand being enveloped by a moist paw. The German's squinty eyes were busying themselves about in the lower region of his visual field in an attempt to capture his attention. But still R. resisted without knowing why, and shifted his glance imprudently to the red-haired woman. Once he had looked at her, his eyes lost their power of motion completely and forced him to remain locked in his gaze. Her face was still smudged with lipstick.

'I had a feeling that her slovenliness was intentional,' R. thought. 'Poor woman, she mustn't have a lot of friends. Otherwise somebody would have advised her to abandon that style, surely.'

Abstracting from her material appearance, however, an onlooker would have been struck by her dignified expression. The smile she was offering to R. was quite unlike her former hostility. It was a programmatic smile sketched under the constraint of the little German's orders.

A sharp pain rushing through the palm of his hand woke R. from his meanderings and caused him to step back; but the host wouldn't release his grip, and R. was only able to pull himself out with great effort.

'Jesus Christ!' R. cried, stupefied. On his injured hand he noticed four little red holes dripping with fresh blood. The German had buried his nails into his skin.

'Do you or do you not want to proceed with the interview?' asked his attacker with a smile of dazzling serenity rendered artificial by the grave tone of his voice. Evidently he had not enjoyed being ignored, but that emotion didn't transpire.

R.'s first impulse had been to kick the German to the ground, bite his fingers off and gouge his eyes out. Few things were as likely to make him lose his mind as the feeling of having suffered an injustice, especially when it came in the form of a physical assault. But in that situation the stakes were so high, and a misstep so easily made, that he forced himself to restrain his impulse.

'I do want to proceed, and I am confident that I will prove this to you very soon,' R. said in a firm voice.

'Proof, you say?' the German darted back with a stillborn laugh, his mouth opening wide to reveal a row of milk teeth. 'Very good then, very good,' he continued in his juvenile voice, nodding to himself repeatedly. 'I suppose we are ready to begin the next stage. Do you have any objections?' he asked, glancing back in the direction of his colleagues.

Both of them shook their heads in silence. They would hardly have been less excited by a remark about the weather.

With a gesture imitating the jotting down of a sentence into a notepad but which was, this time, only performed by his hands, the German slowly turned back and addressed R. in a tone of a gentle warning: 'As we head inside the office, I will ask you to keep silent until a member of the committee authorises you to speak. This is according to the rules of protocol. I will not deny that I have found it pompous and unnecessary at times to follow this template, but it was established very long ago, many decades before any of us started working here. I'm sure you are aware that the more secretive types of institutions tend to lean heavily on protocol. Mastery of the rules and symbols we operate by serves as a signal to the other members that one is not an informant.'

Noticing that R. hadn't been thrown off balance by his note of warning, the German patted him softly on the shoulder and walked him through the door.

'I want to insist on these rules, you see, because what you are about to witness might catch you off-guard. For this I want to apologise pre-emptively, as it were. However, mastery over one's emotions is a skill that we must test in each of our candidates.'

On that word of warning he pushed the door open. Inside the office the big oval table was occupying most of the space. There was barely enough room to pull the chairs back from under it. The mere act of sitting down appeared to require a range of acrobatics that R., stiff as a log of wood, didn't have within his skillset. In the middle of the ceiling, two long bars of neon lights shone a subdued, greenish white reminiscent of the atmosphere of an old morgue.

And yet the environment was also very clean, to the point of sterility. It was permeated down to the smallest particles with a ruthless, technological ideal which R. could breathe but not understand. Opposite the glass wall that overlooked the outside corridor, a barely finished dark grey wall ran for ten meters before meeting the glass wall at a sharp angle. Only at that point did R. realise that the room was shaped like a diamond.

'Look at the back of the room, Mr. C, close to where the walls meet,' said the German.

The peculiar layout of the room, combined with the weak strength of the lights, made it difficult for R. to make out the exact details of his environment. It took his eyes another few minutes to get fully used to the half-darkness.

At the meeting of the two walls R. noticed the figure of a man sitting on a chair. His head was looking down at the floor, not held by his hands. Until a moment earlier the living object at the other end of the room had been concealed by the table; but now R. was able to slowly examine the crooked body shaking nervously against the chair. His arms couldn't be seen, so R. approached closer.

Suddenly he let out a gasp of horror. The stranger was tied up to the chair. R. still couldn't see the legs but he guessed that those were tied up, too. The shocking visual impressions sharpened R.'s sense of sight even further as he felt himself become hypervigilant; gradually he managed to make out the stranger's facial features.

The man, who was bald, had absurdly prominent crow's feet around the corners of his eyes. 'He must be quite old,' R. thought. But paradoxically, his forehead was not very wrinkled. It seemed as if the weight of years had fallen on his eyes – as if he had experienced too much of life's tragedies and grown old at unnatural speed because of it.

R.'s own terror was nothing compared to what he saw in the man's haggard look. It was a look of despair mixed with dread and fatigue, whose gaze had lost the ability to rest anywhere for more than a few seconds. Opened wide and never blinking, the eyes kept scanning the room frantically but without apparent purpose. They were shrieking what the man's mouth couldn't shriek because of the layer of tape that muted it.

The stranger's anxious gaze crossed paths with R.'s and paused for a while. R.'s couldn't tell whether the man was curious or simply too exhausted to look any further. For what felt like an eternity the two men stared at each other in silence, encircled by the creeping shadows of the members of the jury. At a leisurely pace they took their seats around the table—the German at the end of the table near the entrance, less than two meters away from R., while the red-haired woman and the man with the eagle eyes sat on the two opposite sides.

'There is no need to read despite the lines for now, Mr. C. Please sit down,' said the head of the jury, smiling with authority. 'Why don't you go over to the other end of the table? There should be a free chair waiting for you. This will give you the opportunity to give a warm welcome to our guest. Obviously you have not recognised him yet. Not that there is anything surprising about that. The Diamond Room was designed to allow the candidates to take notice of their guests without quite recognising them from a distance. I have been told that this creates an eerie feeling. Would you agree?'

R. didn't answer. This didn't surprise the head interviewer in the least. 'It is fascinating to know that the most human feelings can be conjured so easily by artificial contrivances,' he continued. 'But I would not want to digress too much. Please make your way to the other end of the table and greet your guest before we proceed with the interview.'

Once again R. gave no reply, but he understood immediately that there was no going back. He could feel the threat of attack printed on the faces of the committee members. He could measure, even with his back turned on them, the rapidity with which their looks had changed from sullenness to defiance. The old man in particular, armed with his appalling eyes, stared at the nape of his neck in a manner that chilled his bones. All around the room R. heard the loud cracking of knuckles.

'I will take my seat now,' R. said in a neutral voice.

He had only a short distance to cover but the ridiculous narrowness of the passage between the wall and the row of chairs slowed him down considerably, and he nearly tripped several times. The chairs turned out to be extremely heavy; R. was barely able to push them out of his way.

The red-haired woman was greatly amused by that sight. 'Look at the little boy, he's struggling! If only you hadn't doubted my story,' she chuckled, licking the marks of lipstick off her top lip.

Underneath her jeering her spirit of vengeance hadn't died away. She was in no mood to let R. pass behind her with ease; on the contrary, she pushed her chair back a little and stretched her arms so far behind that she almost slapped R.'s cheek with the back of her hand. This only amused her further, and the loud, gurgling chuckles followed in succession.

As he slipped behind the laughing woman laboriously, his back stuck to the wall like a chameleon failing to blend with the background, R. was assailed by two additional pains. Scraping the wall he realised that its surface was not smooth but grainy, as if covered with spikes. Underneath his shirt he felt blood and sweat dripping down his back from the scratches. But that source of discomfort was made worse by another, even more unpleasant one, which originated from the body of the laughing woman. As he snaked his way behind her, R. was overwhelmed by a horrible stench wafting from her neck. He felt his stomach harrowing him with retching urges. The woman, who was still mocking him, smelt like a rotting corpse.

'That's why she puts on such an absurd amount of makeup and drowns herself in perfume,' he reflected with horror. 'She's been concealing her true nature.'

The force of disgust made him jump forward in an attempt to get away from her. He succeeded but struck his shinbone violently against the leg of a chair nearby, though strangely the pain of that collision, which ought to have been excruciating, was softened by the previous combination of pains he had just suffered.

With effort R. grabbed the back of the chair. Sighing, he realised that he had no strength left to push it aside. Feeling that the pain in his shin was beginning to feel more acute, he raised his head slowly to inspect the chair. At that moment he let out a long, shrill shriek and fell backwards, nearly breaking his neck on the edge of the table.

The prisoner with the searching eyes was tied up to the chair. He was now staring at R. with an intensity that rarefied the air and made breathing almost impossible. His eyes bordered by crow's feet expressed a mix of supplication and warning, as if he were trying to convey the order: 'Save me! Run away!'

The man's wriggling body was no help in moving the chair; on the contrary, the weight of his excited bones now made the enterprise entirely hopeless.

'You still don't recognise him, do you?' asked the mechanical voice of the German, echoing against the walls from the other end of the room. 'Get a little closer. Don't be timid, he is not in a position to hurt you. Come on, get a little closer!' he thundered in unison with his colleagues.

Gripped by fear, R. crept back slowly to the stranger's chair. The man's hands and feet were fastened to the arms and legs of the chair with intricate knots.

'The work of a professional,' R thought. From where he was the light issued from a new angle, which helped him uncover what had thus far remained hidden from him. He could now scrutinise the whole, coherent appearance of the man on the chair. He noticed the slightly crooked shape of the nose and the cauliflower ears. Underneath the tape that covered the mouth he was even able to divine the chin redone years before by plastic surgery. The thin crown of hair that remained scattered around the scalp was still black.

Suddenly everything came into focus and struck R. with the force of a lightning bolt. The man sitting in front of him was his father.

'Do not touch him,' commanded the voice of the German, who saw that R. had lifted the veil off the identity of his guest. 'This is another of our rules, which I should have specified earlier. Make your way to your own chair now.'

His eyes still riveted by the gaunt, awful figure of his father, R. slowly made his way to the chair and took his seat. Was he shocked, horrified, or indifferent? For the moment he could not tell. There was no way of knowing, and he hated that feeling. All he could feel was a sudden pang of overwhelming fatigue. He felt like he hadn't slept in years. With a downcast look bereft of all vitality, he let his elbows fall on the sides of the table.

On the other side the German's smile shone a new light reaching all the way across the table. 'You are showing remarkable resilience, Mr. C.', he said, glowing with satisfaction. 'We are impressed, and frankly a little surprised, by your performance. Most of the candidates who make their way to the Diamond Room suffer a debilitating blow at this juncture, but you—you haven't even lost consciousness! If only you knew how many whimpering little boys and girls we have had to interview today… They all fell abjectly to their knees and begged us to free the person on the chair. Needless to say, we had to eliminate them straightaway. To beg is to lose, if you will. This is an old proverb which originates from within the walls of the organisation. The founder himself came up with it.'

Noticing that R. hadn't quite recovered from his state of shock, the German continued his little exposé with perfect naturalness. 'The simple yet unassailable reason why people fail the interview is that the extreme susceptibility of the human psyche conditions it to abhor the unexpected. Any surprise, any slight deviation from expectation, is a covert source of anxiety for most people. By setting in place a system which facilitates the largest possible deviation, the interview effectively guarantees that only the best will remain standing. It is a formidably robust formula, and one which has enabled us to fill our ranks with the most exceptional personalities the continent has to offer. I am not merely referring to cognitive ability, but also to mental endurance and strength of will. The question that remains to be answered is whether you, Mr. C., possess all three qualities. However, before we proceed, you may wish us to elucidate a number of grey areas. Do you have any queries?'

Due to his befuddled mental condition, R. had not managed to assimilate the finer elements of that lengthy speech. Luckily, in his mind the hardest fragment to break was the synthetic element; so despite his state of extreme confusion he managed to reduce the content of the interviewer's words down to its essential parts.

When he had achieved that, he tried to look in front of him; but what felt like an invisible piece of elastic band, binding his neck to the neck of his father, kept directing his eyes back to the man on the chair.

In a moment of clarity R. realised that his best chance to keep himself and his father out of trouble was to be on his best behaviour with the panel. But when he inferred from that realisation that it would probably entail their prolonged psychological torture inside the Diamond Room, his spirits wavered and dread overcame him.

'I would like to know why my father is here,' R. queried weakly. 'Why is he here, and why did you tie up him to that chair? I thought my father was in Corsica.'

At this the man with the eagle eyes couldn't contain himself and laughed uproariously. 'He's asking about Corsica!' he cried, beating his chest to let the air come out. 'The old myth of a son's love for his father is shattered!'

'Corsica is charming place,' retorted the red-haired woman, admonishing her neighbour. 'And I don't see why people shouldn't be allowed to associate their loved ones with the places they visit. Maybe this young man's father feels very attached to Corsica, so much so that he conceives the two, father and island, as both sides of the same person.'

'You always have to cover everything with intellectual veneer,' the old man complained, loudly but without conviction. As a consequence of his intimate knowledge of the lady's quirks, her reactions had become entirely unsurprising to him, and thus flavourless.

Suddenly both sides were reduced to silence by the raising of the German's arm.

'I could make the answer to your question very complicated or very easy,' he began, his irises almost touching each other through the bridge of his nose. 'However, in view of what you have just been through, I will opt for the simpler narrative. I have said this before: what we want to do now is test your mental endurance. This includes not only your resilience to various types of stress, but also your ethical outlook and the consistency with which you apply it. Your father is your guest because the smallest amount of research into your background makes it plain that he is the most disruptive element in your life.

You think that the best and the worst in you originate from his treatment of you when you were young. You both love and hate him. Very recently you expressed the wish to 'confront' him—those were your own words, as I'm sure you remember. I may equally assume that you are familiar with the Freudian concept of the 'killing of the father'. Well, the conclusion of the syllogism appears obvious: you aspire to kill your father in some way. What if I told you that we, the interview committee appointed by the organisation, had decided to help you with this endeavour? Our help does not and cannot consist in forcing you to perform an immoral act, but in facilitating it. We can contribute to a speeding up of the process, if you will.'

The German pointed to the corner of the table directly to R.'s left, close to the wall of glass.

'You cannot see it distinctly because of the refraction of light through the glass, but to your left there is a dagger. Feel free to inspect it, pick it up, and maybe consider how it may be put to good use. From now on it is all up to you, Mr. C. We shall be merely observing and taking notes.'

R. carefully examined the dagger. It was short but sharp and almost transparent, as if made of crystal. With a hesitating hand R. caressed its handle softly. That dagger and its strange, ethereal appearance looked to him like an object made of dreams and nightmares. It was outside of space and time like the black corridor downstairs. The greenish beams of the neon lights were reflected in the blade in a manner that defied the laws of physics; the beams were sucked inside its inert body, prisoners in their turn to a mute fortress living in neither past nor future but in the present—a cold, permanent present that was maybe not the present at all but a timeless eternity.

R. had completely lost any sense of time. He had not the least idea how many hours had passed since his departure from the Petal Building; perhaps it was merely minutes. With a sigh he looked at his naked wrist and longed for his forgotten watch. What was he supposed to do? What did the committee really expect from him? Kill his father? Refuse to kill him? 'I might as well play a game of dice!' he thought, anxious and helpless.

R. already knew that he had no intention to kill his father. He was at that moment unable to conjure up the thought because it seemed so foreign, so unthinkable indeed. He had only been able to picture his thirst for violent revenge figuratively, by means of vivid images, but never physically. A short-lived counsellor from the distant past had made him conscious of that fact. R. now recalled the man's paradoxical smile and wrinkled brow hiding in its trenches a blend of curiosity and repulsion. 'A patient should never feel judged by his counsellor,' R. had thought before dismissing him.

An obscure sense of duty, not unlike the way people feel when mechanically they greet utter strangers in the lift, eventually caused R. to stand up and walk slowly to the corner of the table, where the dagger was resting with its rainbow of imprisoned beams.

'I must do something. It is time,' he reasoned. But now the invisible force stopped him from looking in the direction of his father. Not only his body but his sense of right and wrong—his entire moral compass was vaporised along with his means of measuring the time. The call of conscience had become the shadow of a whisper to him.

'A hint of indecisiveness!' the German almost sang from the other end of the room, taking out his notepad and writing some notes into it with a shake of the head.

The old man knocked his elbow violently against the table. 'Indecisiveness!' he shouted in the direction of his boss. 'Can't you see that he's not the right fit for us? He's not indecisive, he's lost!'

The German raised his hand to reduce his colleague to silence. 'I haven't finished writing down my notes,' he said, grimacing. 'Do not let me lose the thread of my reasoning.'

The admonishment proved so successful that within a few seconds the man with the eagle eyes had returned to his suppressed mutterings and occasional sidelong glances at the red-haired woman. The woman, for her part, was gaping at R. wide-eyed, as if the uncertainty that was traversing him was causing a malfunctioning of the power supply that fed her bodily movements.

'The boy is doing fine. Look now, he's standing up! He's caressing the handle of the dagger!' she exclaimed with her distinctive, lipstick-smudged smile. 'His decision-making is improving!' Then she followed up with a somewhat incoherent diatribe about how the cowardice of the father was much more shocking to her than the son's indecision.

The old man laughed his raucous laugh. 'Now you're defending the boy,' he teased. 'What about the time when you wanted to gouge his eyes out?'

The laws of physics were so bent in that room that when the old man delivered another powerful knock of the elbow against the table, the noise of the impact was heard without vibration. And even the noise, as soon as it had issued from the impact, had been instantly depleted of its force, like the desperate cry of an immured man.

'Instinct and feelings supersede logic,' the red-haired woman retorted with renewed confidence, feeling safe under the benevolent eyes of the German. There was so much latent power in those barely functioning eyes. It was obvious that the others were afraid of him. All he had to do was hint at a vague displeasure with the manner of their conduct, and immediately all would be set right.

'With me it's all about instinct,' the woman continued with caution. 'I never make decisions based on logic alone because I don't trust the kinds of judgement that follow from it. It's the same with that boy over there,' she said, pointing her bony index finger at R. 'My gut tells me that he's about to do something very surprising and impressive, but we have to be patient and give him the chance to do so. He is so young.'

The German smiled and nodded in silence. The old man, who from a corner of his eye kept discreetly scanning for his superior's moods, noticed it and was forced to nod, too.

Bolstered by those remarks and almost touched by the good will that was shown to him, R. brought his arm down and grabbed the handle of the dagger. When it turned out to be light as a feather he could not repress a gasp of astonishment. Inquisitively he pressed his fingers against the handle like a surveyor exploring a new land. 'Incredible,' he thought.

The German was still smiling and nodding at him with his trademark composure, but now the red-haired woman was also caressing him with a whole new pair of eyes. The man with the eagle eyes had never looked more defeated. With his face buried deep inside his shirt collar, he was still muttering unintelligible sounds and nervously clenching his fists. For the first time it occurred to R. that he was perhaps headed towards success. 'If it's two against one, I have a chance of making it,' he observed to himself.

*****

The last phase of the interview had begun. Feeling a surplus of strength now coursing through his veins, R. snatched the dagger and glided effortlessly towards the man on the chair. With newfound detachment he scrutinised his father's lowered head and felt a pang of annoyance that he easily drove away. Not flinching for a second, he poked the tip of the dagger against his father's large forehead.

'What are you here for?' R. murmured in his father's ear. 'Do you always have to meddle with my affairs? How much did they pay you to play this sickening mind game?'

But his father did not reply, and even refused to look at him.

'Maybe they didn't have to pay you. Wishing for my success has always been a pretext for you to undermine me,' R. continued, sensing his anger rise. 'Well, you've done a damn good job of it, let me tell you. I have not the least idea what to do. I'm almost certain that you're on their side, but what if you're not? If I throw the dagger away now and tell them I've seen through their game, because I know what you're capable of, what if they tell me I was wrong? You have to understand that I need this job. I need to succeed, no matter the cost. Do you understand what I'm saying?'

But still his father did not reply, and would not look at him.

'Look at me, for God's sake!' R. shouted desperately. 'I know you can hear me! Look at me!'

No matter his efforts, he obtained no response. He repeated his plea dozens of times and each time his voice was raised a little higher, until he had to pause and give a rest to his vocal chords.

His last attempt had been a hysterical shriek delivered at such an unnaturally high pitch that it greatly amused the man with the eagle eyes. 'The little baby is crying because his father won't notice him! Isn't that endearing?'

'Will you shut up for once? I'm telling you he's about to do something very surprising,' said the red-haired woman, threatening her neighbour with a display of her claws.

R. refrained from looking back at the committee because he knew that he was failing. All the while, however, he could still feel the firm, Teutonic hand of the head interviewer being raised here and there at intervals with the expert movements of a classical conductor. It was that deft, supple hand, more than the defensive instinct he was feeling to prove the old man wrong, which was now guiding his own hand from the other side of the table and letting it rub the edge of the blade against his father's temples.

'For the last time, father, I order you to look at me,' R. said with an involuntary lisp.

His father raised his head slightly, but not enough to look into R.'s eyes. He had lowered his head at the sight of R.'s approach a few minutes earlier, perhaps hours earlier, and had kept his chin pressed against his chest ever since; consequently this new movement of his, faint as it might have been, was taken by his son as a sign of incoming submission. R. took advantage of the space freed up above his father's chest to lightly press the tip of the blade upwards against his chin.

'Higher,' R. insisted, with a little poke of the blade that proved immediately successful. 'Who knows what the fear of impending death won't make us do,' he thought. But when at last he was able to stare into his father's eyes, he was horrified to discover in them a bottomless well of malice. He knew that his father became almost slit-eyed when he smiled as a result of the power of pressure caused by the stretching of the cheeks, and at that moment those eyes were so much like slits that R. wasn't even able to distinguish the pair of brown rises that he knew they concealed.

His father was laughing at him. Had he been biding his time on purpose, waiting for the most opportune moment to manifest his derision?

Dumbstruck by that unexpected sight, R. dropped the dagger on the floor and took a frightened step backwards. He realised that he was out of breath and that his heart was again pounding inside his chest.

'What the hell are you waiting for? Kill him! Pick up the damn dagger and kill him!' shouted the man with the eagle eyes.

But R. did not listen. He had no strength left in him to do anything else than keep staring, now from a safer distance, at his father's strangely laughing eyes.

From that new angle R. noticed a hidden anomaly in his facial features; he saw it with his eyes but couldn't have described it in words. He had seen his father smile a thousand times and through each of those memories a common thread ran which made those smiles what they were—smiles whose mould had been imprinted on his father's face like the marks on the trunk of an old tree. But now R. failed to find that thread, and his inability to unveil its familiar presence left him feeling more helpless than when he had realised that his father was laughing at him.

At first R. did not understand the peculiar nature of those feelings. He could trust nothing else than the stinging sensation of a burgeoning emotion, which was trying to tell him a truth that no medical instrument, no mathematical formula would have been able to reveal. His father's smiling eyes lacked the common thread which ran through his past smiles; that little fragment of his father's essence was missing; and though R. was incapable of describing that essence in words, he found the pain of its absence agonising.

Then another thought occurred to him and pained him in some unknown location of his body. He remembered the time when, having just turned fifteen, he had heard about Peter's death. Peter was the son of John, his father's closest friend. R. had always admired that boy and had looked up him as a role model. Peter was adventurous and fun-loving, and so full of life and kindness that it was impossible not to love him. With the power of a young man's heart R. had felt grateful for his friendship. Secretly he dreamt of developing with Peter a relationship that mirrored his father's friendship with John. And for many years, much to R.'s delight, things seemed headed in that direction. The two boys' opposite personalities completed each other so flawlessly that it was clear each one relished to access in the other, even if for short periods of time, what he himself lacked.

One cold winter night R. answered a call from Guy, another acquaintance of his father's. Guy was a greedy nurse whom his father didn't like very much, but who was a close friend and distant relative of John.

'Peter had a terrible accident,' Guy said. 'He is dead.'

With watery eyes and a heavy heart, R. learned that Peter, who had wanted to try out his new scooter, had been hit by a truck on the outskirts of ___.

'He didn't suffer,' Guy said. Days later, R. learned that the impact of the crash had shattered Peter's ribcage to pieces.

In the months that followed the accident, it transpired that Peter's father had completely cut ties with Guy, putting an abrupt end to decades of friendship, for reasons obscure to everybody except one person: R.'s father. R. made several attempts to uncover the mystery.

'I cannot talk about it,' his father would reply.

John never recovered from his son's death. He spent years doing practically nothing else than smoking and drinking. Soon enough an aggressive form of cancer had consigned him to his grave. R. was amazed to witness the devotion with which his father supported the twice bereft family, having already spent a seemingly infinite number of hours by John's side at the hospital. Yet paradoxically, John's death seemed to have relaxed in his father's eyes the promise he had once made of keeping the secret. Nearly a decade later, during a casual walk along the shore of Lake ___, R. revisited the topic of the severed ties between John and Guy. That time his father breathed a deep sigh of relief.

'You may not know this,' his father said, 'but Guy was heading the team of life supporters who tried to revive Peter. He himself made the final attempt. When Guy told John that his son had died, he apparently smiled in a strange, distorted way. He was almost laughing. John never forgot about the look on Guy's face. It was like his failed attempt at reviving Peter had filled him with joy.'

As he recounted those horrible events, R.'s father imitated the distorted smile that Guy had made. It was a nervous and unnatural smile, in no way malicious, which had obviously been a symptom of extreme stress and fatigue. But to John the explanation was diametrically opposite. The way in which the events had unleashed their cruel sequence had climaxed with the smile on Guy's face and his horrible laughing eyes.

'You are afraid,' R. whispered, looking at the man tied up on the chair. But he was not able to understand his own words. The idea that his father was afraid of him was such a foreign one that his mind wasn't ready to accept it.

Instinctively he let his head drop in his hands and pressed his temples in a desperate attempt to make sense of the new situation. Afraid! Did his father even know the meaning of that word?

R. realised at that moment that deep down the bottom of his soul he had never seriously believed that his father might experience such a thing as fear. So when the fact of that fear was revealed to him with the artless spontaneity of memory, when in its sudden association of the present with the past it pushes forward a conclusion never deliberated, R. was thrown off balance by an invisible agent creeping beneath the layer of his will. He suffered pangs of anguish through his whole body all the way to his trembling feet.

The raucous jeering of the man with the eagle eyes shook the Diamond Room once again. He said something about calling a doctor, overtly mocking the paleness of R.'s face.

'He's about to have a seizure!' the man's guttural voice echoed around the room.

R. was irritated by the old man's tricks to such an unbearable degree that he felt his nerves squirming underneath his skin. With great effort he collected himself and looked at him in the face. R.'s eyes were glowing with a strange light; there was no fire left in them, but instead a piercing, frozen glare. The entire committee saw those eyes and felt greatly alarmed by the sight.

'He is afraid, but not I,' R. said, pointing at his father. 'You have failed at making me afraid.'

Both the old man and the red-haired lady were baffled by those words. They looked at each other with raised eyebrows and faint jitteriness in the limbs. The German too was speechless, but his speechlessness had a different source. He was no longer taking notes, but instead was delicately rubbing his hands and staring back at R. with a beatific smile.

R. did not wait for the committee to come up with a more articulate reaction. With slow, deliberate movements he got up from his chair and made his way to the door.

'I'm afraid I'm no longer interested in the position,' he said, looking sideways at the German. 'Thank you for your time.' And on those words he exited the Diamond Room.

'What do we do with him?' the old man asked his superior, dumb with confusion. In answer the German only raised his arm in objection. The beatific smile was still buried into his face, but by now the utter stillness of it looked artificial, like the involuntary final position of a broken engine.

*****

On his way out R. felt a strong urge to urinate. By chance a double door that he hadn't noticed before, situated not very far from the door to the black corridor, presented itself to him. He pushed through it and noted with satisfaction that his gut had been right: it was the men's bathroom.

As he relieved himself he couldn't get rid of a thought that was still bothering him. Although he felt largely satisfied that by taking his leave he had broken the committee's spell, he was still under the impression that the task remained incomplete. A central element was missing from it, but he couldn't identify what it was, and that realisation frustrated and concerned him.

He had barely zipped up his fly when he heard the sound of the double door being opened behind him, followed by rapid, clumsy steps. He heard someone breathing heavily and grunting around the corner, until at last the sound of steps stopped. He could almost smell that breath now.

'It is not yet finished,' said the man with the eagle eyes. 'You left too early.'

'And what exactly remains unfinished?' R. asked, not turning back.

'Your father. You have not finished him.'

'I'm afraid I don't understand.'

'The head interviewer was very clear. You have to kill him.'

'I think you are very much afraid of the head interviewer.'

'That may be so,' whispered the old man. 'But I have experience with those interviews, and I can tell you that if you don't kill him, you won't succeed. Your little display of strength at the end was impressive, but you have still come short.'

R. turned around and looked at the old man with a perplexed expression.

'But I have killed him.'

'What do you mean?' the old man asked, sensing terror overcoming him.

'I saw that he was afraid of me. That is all I wanted to achieve.'

The old man fell on his knees, panting heavily.

'But that… is not real killing,' he said, bursting into tears.

'But he was not my real father,' R. replied coolly.

The old man was now fully prostrated in front of R. 'I know,' he murmured. Still panting heavily, he felt caressed by the strange vibration of the dagger being lifted above his head.

R. stroked the old man's mass of white hair with his free hand. 'It is time to bring the interview to an end,' R. said.

'I know,' the old man replied.

And it ended.